The Lo

Gunman's Past

By
Sam Settle

Charlie Berg

Printed in the United States of America

Table of Contents

Few Unsolicited Testimonials for my books

By **Don & Sheila**

☆☆☆☆☆ "SS.. has. penned the third novel in the Cooper ride for vengence. Cooper returns home ready to begin the fight against those who killed his family. Cooper uses his prowess with guns and teaches the town members how to shoot for the final showdown. When the town is ready to fight the bad me they take a break to rest and wait for the return of the gang. This is an excellent read for the genre.....DEHS"

By **Randy Reminder**

☆☆☆☆☆ " This book was hard to put down and I found myself reading far later in the night than I intended but oh my it was good. There is potential for a series of books being written around the characters introduced in this first book and in fact I went back to amazon to see if there were more!"

By **raliquin**

☆☆☆☆☆ " Well written and good storyline. Easy reading with believable events. Looking forward to continuing reading more books from this author."

By **Kindle Customer**

☆☆☆☆☆ Great story, great characters, waiting for the next episode.

Sam Settle is a great writer, gives us lots of action and characters that are interesting and believable will continue to read his books

By **Ernie**

☆☆☆☆☆ Non-stop

Non-stop action keeps you turning page's wondering what happens next.Impossible To put down definitely a page turner keeps you wanting more.

FREE GIFT

Just to say thanks for checking my works I like to gift you

100% FREE!

Please GO TO

http://coolromancepublishing.com/gift/

And get your FREE gift

Thanks for being such a wonderful client.

Chapter One

Charlie Berg noticed the mountains to the west looming larger as he headed south. Their jagged white peaks were soaring above the clouds. As much as Charlie loved adventure, he'd probably never scale those peaks. He was glad they were there, though, because they were his marker to keep going in the proper direction. This was necessary because, at times, he veered away from the river.

When he'd left Casper, Wyoming, Staff, Mel, Trixie and the other friends he left behind had urged him to build a raft and float down the river. It would take him straight to Nebraska, which was where he wanted to end up eventually. Charlie had reason to believe his sister Betsy was there, and her safety was at issue. He decided, however, to go overland, because floating down the river would mean leaving behind his horse Kip.

Kip was a chestnut horse who stood average height, and most didn't see him as anything special. The thing was, he was a unique animal, with more loyalty and courage than most people Charlie knew. Charlie didn't choose Kip; rather, the horse had chosen him. His good friend and father-figure

Staff had brought the horse home when he worked on the railroad. A man had died while working with him, and had left behind his horse. Staff had it tied up in front of his cabin until he could sell it.

But the animal seemed to resist any new owner. He bucked and pounded his hoof hard on the ground when anyone approached him, making a display that Charlie and everyone else couldn't help but notice. People had told Staff he should shoot the unruly horse, because he would be nothing but trouble, but Staff's heart was too big to do that.

Charlie was feeling bold one day, so he approached the horse. The normally unruly animal calmed immediately, and their bond was evident from the get-go.

The horse became Kip, the name from a book read to him by his mother. Kip hadn't shown the slightest bit of aggression from that day forward.

"I think this is a good enough spot to rest for the night. Don't you agree, Augie?" Charlie asked his loyal dog that most people thought was a wolf.

The dog didn't answer exactly, but he cocked his head to the left, which was good enough.

"I wouldn't trade this view for a roof and four walls. Maybe because I'm young, but I don't see my preference for sleeping under the stars going away," Charlie mused.

Charlie was only nineteen, but in those years, he'd done a lot of living. He had cared for two sick parents and eventually buried them, and made friends with Indians and enemies of thieves. Now his mission was to rescue his sister Betsy from a bad situation in Nebraska. He hoped the journey to find Betsy would be filled with adventure. He didn't know exactly where she was—all he knew was she was last heard from in Nebraska, which was pretty darn big.

Betsy was the last of Charlie's family, as far as he knew. Charlie's two older brothers, Al and BJ, were also long gone. They had run from Casper because they'd tired of living in the shadow of Bill Berg. They were hotheads who Charlie never got to know as men, and now they were likely dead.

Charlie's ears perked at the sound of an unfamiliar call. It wasn't like any bird he had known, and it sounded almost human.

The sound came again, and this time Charlie made out the words. "Hellooo…"

It surely wasn't a bird, unless birds downriver had learned human words, which would be a shame. Their voices were perfect the way they were.

Charlie responded, "Hello, I'm not going to shoot, and my dog Augie won't bite. Come on out and show your face, because I'm at a disadvantage. You can see me, but I can't lay eyes on you."

After some rustling in the brush, a short-bearded man revealed himself. "I took a risk thinking you and your dog would be the friendly sort. I was watching you and saw the way ya gave a gander at them mountains. You seem like a mindful man."

"I'm Charlie Berg, on my way through on the trail. I called Casper, Wyoming, home for many years. Now I don't belong to any town in particular," Charlie said.

The man had a jug of moonshine and offered a sip, but Charlie turned him down.

"Yer a wandering cowboy like me. Are you looking to get somewhere in particular?" the man asked.

Charlie nodded. "Eventually. I have to tend to business in Nebraska. What's your name, stranger? It will be an even trade, because you already know mine."

“My name is Linc. I forget it sometimes, because I’m by myself mostly, so I never hear it spoken.”

“That’s a fine name, Linc. How long have you been by yourself, living the wandering life?” Charlie asked.

"I lost count. I had me a wife—a real fine lady. Desperados killed her, and I walked away from life in the city. I left my house and just walked away. And I kept walking, then I arrived here. It must be a long time ago, because I noticed my hands are creased and the hair I pull from my head is grey. How old do you suppose I am?"

"Hard to say, but old enough to be my daddy, and I'm nineteen," Charlie said.

“Hmm… nineteen is the age I was when I started wandering. I have some advice for you, Charlie Berg. Wanna listen?”

"Sure. I never turn down listening, because my momma used to say that's how ya learn," Charlie said.

“Smart lady,” Linc said. “My advice is never to be alone so long that it starts to feel normal. Don’t get too comfortable being alone, because then it's hard to be around people when you need em. My wife and I had a son, but he don't want nothing to do with me. An aunt and uncle raised him. They became his mama and papa… guess I deserve to be an outcast. I have nowhere or no one to go home to, and it gets perty lonely. The freedom is great, but when yer old and rickety like me, you'd love four walls and a roof. A soft blanket would be nice, too."

Charlie noticed how the man's words echoed his earlier thoughts, and felt a slight shiver. "I figured I'd go along the mountains, which I plan to keep to the west. Heard many a story of the most capable man trying to cross and never being heard from again," Charlie said.

"That's true. I tried once, but wasn't prepared for the wind and snow. Got its own kinda weather up yonder. I suggest you head to Burley—you'll run into it if you keep moving south. Got some nice folks down that way, but your usual number of scoundrels too. Burley ain't different than most towns in the Wild West." Linc looked at Augie, who was onto a critter. "What's that he got?"

"I think it's dinner." Charlie laughed.

Charlie and Linc cooked rabbit over the fire as they swapped stories. It was obvious Linc was itching to talk to a human being—he had a lot of stories. When Charlie opened his eyes the next morning, Linc was gone. He wouldn't be the last lonesome cowboy Charlie would encounter, and he hoped with each one he'd get a nugget of advice. He'd also be open to advising, if anyone was looking after it.

Charlie packed up, whistled for Augie, and rode Kip towards Burley, Colorado.

Chapter Two

Yapping prairies dogs and mountain goats were a source of constant amusement to Augie as Kip traversed the rugged crags. They moved from grasslands, which covered short distances, to rock-covered hills, which covered much of the landscape. Winds were starting to blow colder as they came off the mountains, and Autumn was beginning to show as the leaves were starting to fall from any tree that wasn't a pine. Charlie had passed a wagon or two, so he felt as if a town was coming close.

Finally, Charlie came across a small river—probably an offshoot of the Platte. A man was dipping his pole in the waters, so he stopped to ask some questions.

"Hello, sir," Charlie said.

The skinny man looked frightened and turned to Charlie. He was wearing a collar, which meant he was a man of God. "You scared me, son, or maybe it was that wolf traveling with you. Did you know a wolf was following you?"

Charlie chuckled. "It's my dog, Augie. He gets mistaken for a wild animal all the time. I didn't mean to scare ya, Pastor. I was just wondering if I was heading towards a town?"

The man looked confused for a moment. "Max? I haven't seen you in the church for weeks. I see you've lost your way. Do you remember me? Pastor Matthew."

Charlie shook his head. "I'm afraid you're mistaken. I'm Charlie Berg, and I was just passing through. I've never come across you in my life. Hear a place called Burley was near here, and I could use some human interaction before I continue my journey."

A smile came over the Pastor's face. "I sure am sorry, Charlie. My eyes make mistakes because my years are getting on. Max was a man working at Harold Turner's ranch, who disappeared just as he seemed to be settling in. Tends to happen here in Burley, which is only here because of the silver mine," Pastor Matthew said. "There isn't silver no more, but the town still stands."

"You answered my question, Pastor. I made a friend on the trail who said Burley was a nice place to stop. You mentioned the Turner Ranch—do you happen to know if they need a ranch hand? I have some money, but I hope to see my sister someday, and I'd like to have something to share with her. She needs help getting out of a bad situation," Charlie said.

"I always find that next to prayer, money helps get out of a bad situation. Harold Turner is a tricky fella—not many know him well. Doesn't come to the church much. Will I see you at church services, Charlie Berg?"

"I'm a Christian man, Pastor, but it's been some time since I walked into a building with a cross on top." Charlie glanced down as he noticed Augie taking a liking to the Pastor, sniffing at his pants legs before rushing off into the brush.

"He must smell my dog, Daisy. She's around here somewhere; must have got scared off, but she'll be back. If it don't work out with Harold, you can always stay with me in the parsonage. It's a fancy word for a shack I keep behind the church."

"I appreciate the offer, and I think meeting you was good fortune, Pastor. I have a good feeling about Burley, Colorado."

Charlie whistled, but Augie didn't appear. Pastor Matthew called Daisy, and she didn't show up either. Even Kip looked a bit concerned, because they had been through losing Augie before. Charlie whistled some more, and finally

Augie came strutting out of the bushes with Daisy prancing close behind. Augie walked with his nose down most of the time, always looking for his next meal. With Daisy behind him, his head was held high, and he was looking regal. Daisy was a shaggy, skinny dog that looked more like an overgrown cat than anything else.

"Looks like Augie made a friend. I'll be seeing you, Pastor," Charlie said as he rode off on Kip. Augie hesitantly followed, stopping every few steps to turn back and look at his new buddy.

With the sun taking its bow behind the jagged peaks to the west, Charlie decided to stop for the night. He didn't want to impose on Harold Turner after dark. He might be mistaken for a thief and have his head shot off, which would be a bad start to his journey. Charlie was in no rush to get to Burley, and Kip would enjoy the chance to rest.

It must have rained where he was now, because holes in the trail were filled with water. They weren't all the way full, but enough to satisfy Kip. As a rule, Charlie didn't let his animals sip from his canteen. If water was around, they'd find it. Keeping it for himself was more important because if he died, they surely would too.

Charlie covered a log with a blanket to make a pillow so he could stargaze in comfort. The moon was about three-fourths full with a gauzy circle that was a sign of fog coming down from the mountain. Soon the cold nights would move in, and suddenly a roof over his head didn't seem like a bad thing. He thought of that offer from the Pastor about staying at his place. Charlie would take him up on it for a few nights if things didn't work out with Harold Turner.

While he was considering the next few weeks, Charlie closed his eyes and fell asleep.

***

“Give me one good reason I shouldn’t shoot you dead.” A man of average size with a mustache and reddish hair pointed a rifle at Charlie’s head. It was not the welcome he had hoped for when he had approached the ranch after a good night’s sleep.

"I can think of a mess of reasons. First one that comes to mind is that I ain't done nothing wrong. I don't know who you are, but I was hoping you were someone who'd give me a job for a spell. If I'm not mistaken, it looks like you have some crops coming ready."

"What the heck, Max? Are you pretending like you don't know me? You owe me money, and I know you was looking around my ranch in places you had no business being."

The man was Harold Turner himself, and once again, Charlie was mistaken for Max.

"My name's Charlie Berg." He took off his hat to display the mop of shaggy hair and smiled. Hopefully, it would prove he wasn't Max. "I've never met you, sir. I just came from Wyoming, passing through on my way to Nebraska."

"You're too far west to be in Nebraska, Charlie," Harold said. His face softened when he realized Charlie was who he claimed to be.

"It's the way I travel, I suppose. I don't go in any particular direction. My destination is important, but for now, I'm in no rush because there are scoundrels who have their eyes out for me. Best to let matters cool before I show up on my sister's doorstep."

"I don't care where you're heading or who the heck your sister is. Any chance the scoundrels will show up making trouble for me?" Harold asked.

"No, they'd be in Nebraska. Too stupid and lazy to follow me here. You got work for me and maybe a stable where I can lay my head?" Charlie asked.

Harold saw Augie and shook his head. "You and the dog come as a package?"

Charlie looked down and petted Augie. "We sure do, but he can sleep in the field. He stays where I tell him to."

“I’m just worried if your wolf will git my livestock,” Harold commented.

Charlie laughed. "He'd rather make friends with your animals. He's not a wolf, by the way, and his name is Augie."

"Good enough, I've got sheep that need shearing, and I'll have a few deer that need gutting, and then the meat hung in the drying shed. That sound like something you’d be interested in?” Harold asked.

“Show me what to do and where I’ll sleep, and I’ll do it.”

"I ain't paying you until the work is done. Did that with Max and he ran off." Harold grumbled.

Sounded to Charlie like Max was quite the scoundrel.

Chapter Three

Like Charlie had asked, Harold found him a place to stay in the stable. It wasn't like most stables in Casper, which were slanted with the shingles sliding off the roof. It was made of sturdy wood and stood up straight like a schoolmarm. Harold had money, probably the most in the town of Burley. Charlie had passed through the town, and it was clear most structures had been built quickly without much thought. He imagined the mine had been dug and found to be full of silver. After that, prospectors had rushed to the place and needed services like a saloon, church, and mercantile.

The place was curious, so Charlie wanted to find out what Harold Turner meant to Burley and what the place meant to him.

Charlie was sitting on a bundle of hay when Harold wandered in. He likely didn't think Charlie would stick around.

"Find everything you need?" Harold said. He was imposing not from size but in the way he stood and his booming voice.

"I found the knives for gutting the carcasses, but they could use some sharpening. I found the salt container for curing the meat, and it's almost empty, so I thought I'd take a ride into town."

"I have an account at the mercantile, and Andy Mercer should be able to take care of ya there. If you hop out of town with my knives and salt, I'll catch you, and it won't be pretty," Harold warned.

"No, sir. I know that happened to you with that Max character. What did he do exactly? You said something about looking in places he shouldn't have."

“Well, Charlie, Max was talking to my girls at the house. They cook, clean, and do favors as I see fit. Those girls are off-limits, and one of em went missing soon after Max left. He's a gifted woodcarver and agreed to carve a grand piece for me. I paid him up-front; he stole money, and that makes him a thief. This is the Wild West, and the sheriff can throw Max in a hole for the rest of his days—if I don’t catch him first."

"Oh, I can tell you for sure that I'd never thieve from you, and I won't go nosing around," Charlie promised.

Harold held a stick that was close to being a log and snapped it in half with his bare hands.

"Good, because I like you, Charlie, and don't want anything bad happening to ya." Harold walked out of the stables as Augie growled and Kip grunted.

Charlie got an odd sense from Harold Turner. He liked Harold enough, but didn’t quite trust him. Charlie realized, though, that he didn’t have to trust everyone, and he’d find out more about the mysterious rancher from folks in town.

Charlie Berg was feeling pretty darn good about himself when he walked through downtown Burley. He was wearing clean clothes and hadn’t slept in the dirt for the first time in weeks. Most would think Charlie was living a rough life by sleeping in the stable, but he didn’t feel that way. His bed of hay was soft, and Harold gave him leftovers from the main house. It was more than he’d asked for. He left Kip tied up under a tree and walked past the saloon to the mercantile.

He pushed open the door, which required effort. It seemed like it hadn’t been opened in a while. The shopkeeper wasn’t behind the counter.

“Hello!” Charlie called out.

A short man with a considerable belly came out from the back room. "Hello. Not too often strangers come into the mercantile. Used to be more, back when silver was pouring out of the mine. What can I do you for?”

"I was told that Andy Mercer could help me with what I need. I'm Charlie Berg, and Harold Turner sent me this way. I'll admit that my being here satisfies a curiosity I have," Charlie said as Augie sat patiently by his side.

"I'm Andy, and I'll say that Harold Turner knowing my name makes me scared," he said.

"Why is that? He didn't say anything bad about you," Charlie asked.

"Harold is the richest man in this part of Colorado, and that includes Denver, which is only a day's ride away. No one can figure out why he stays in Burley. We don't see him in town much, and he never has a smile on his face. Many a newcomer to Burley works for him for a short while before moving on," Andy said. "So, why does Burley make you curious?"

"He's stern, but he don't scare me, and I only plan to be here a short while. As far as being curious goes—I guess I'm just a curious man," Charlie scanned the uneven shelves. It looked as if goods were scarce in Burley, Colorado.

Andy supplied Charlie with plenty of salt and gave him directions to have his knives sharpened by Leo Mackey at the blacksmith's shed, which also served as a tannery. Leo was a jack of all trades who had a similar take on Harold Turner.

After talking to Andy and Leo, Charlie was left with more questions than answers. Harold Turner was a mystery, one that Charlie would wait before passing judgment on. He had been wrong about folks in the past, and so far, Harold hadn't done anything bad to him.

Charlie headed back to the Turner Ranch to get work started. He had skinned plenty of deer for his father back in Casper. He always had leftover parts that he saved for his Shoshoni friend Wenatchee, who remained back in Wyoming. The Indians were known not to waste even the smallest part of an animal. They used bones to make needles and tools. They also ate all the organs of the animal by boiling them and adding roots to make them taste good.

The river ran through the middle of the ranch, so his next piece of work would be moving Harold’s livestock from one side to the other. It would give them access to better grazing for the winter and keep them closer to the barn. Winter was a good time to know where your animals were, because it was the time of year the less hearty died off.

Charlie sighed as the ranch came into sight. He had a lot of work ahead of him before he moved on, and Charlie still had a funny feeling in his belly about Harold Turner.

Chapter Four

A tin cup rattling against a tray was the sound Charlie woke up to as leftover breakfast came to him by a strange young woman. Harold generously shared leftovers from his breakfast table. It was divided between him and the pigs, and Charlie was happy to know the pigs were eating so well. He wondered if they knew what they were eating when they tasted a ham steak. The thought made Charlie chuckle, and the woman delivering the food couldn't help but notice.

“What’s so funny?” the woman asked. She didn’t appear as old as Charlie—maybe as young as fifteen. She covered her mouth as if she regretted speaking.

"Oh, nothing. Thank you for bringing breakfast. I'm not used to being served, and the gesture is beyond kind. I was only thinking about how the pigs feel about eating pig parts. An awful thought to share with a lady, but you asked.”

She chuckled. “I’ve never been called a lady.”

Charlie pushed bread into his mouth and waited until he was finished chewing to speak. “Harold must call you by your name—which is?”

A serious look appeared on her face. "Mr. Turner calls me girl or girl with brown hair. My name is Katherine, but no one uses it much.”

“A lovely name, Katherine,” Charlie said. “Are you Harold’s daughter, or maybe his niece?”

There was a sound from down the hall, and Katherine looked in that direction. She swallowed hard and her smile fell away.

Harold Turner walked into the stable, and she disappeared into the shadows.

"Charlie, I expected you to be hard at work by now. I see storms coming down from the mountains, and I need my cattle on this side of the river. You get salt for curing, and your knives sharpened?"

“Yes, sir. Andy Mercer at the mercantile was a great help, and so was Leo, the blacksmith,” he answered.

Harold nodded. “Good, ‘cause we got a load of work ahead getting these cattle ready. I can supply ‘em some hay for the winter when not much else grows. I also need a headcount so I can figure how many I'm sending to slaughter. I load ‘em on a rail car heading to Kansas and then

Chicago. The work of a successful rancher ain't easy."

He glared at Charlie for a moment. "Did that girl get breakfast to you alright?" he asked, eying the younger man.

Charlie nodded. "Katherine is a nice gal, if a bit skittish."

"Yeah, well, I didn't hire you to make friends, Charlie. Girls around here have work to do just as you, so don't get any ideas," Harold said in his booming voice.

Charlie remained silent. He could tell Harold Turner wasn't the friendly type, and Charlie figured all he wanted out of a person was work. He was gruff, and Charlie could deal with gruff as long as he wasn't breaking the law or hurting anyone.

Charlie had half a dozen horses to choose from to round up cattle, but he skipped them all, deciding that Kip was up to the job. Kip wasn't a cattle horse and Augie not a cattle dog, but they obeyed him, which was half the struggle. Charlie called out a few extra dogs to come along, and out he went.

About a half mile down the river was a bridge built by ranch hands the year before. It was

Charlie's goal to get the cattle to cross the bridge, and then that part of his job would be done.

The first thing Charlie noticed when crossing the bridge was how rickety it was. There was little chance a stampede of cattle could cross the thing without falling into the water. Most would die, and Charlie didn't know how Harold would take the news that Charlie killed his herd. He was sure it wouldn't be positive. He decided to continue downriver until he could find a stretch of river that the cattle could safely cross. Charlie had learned from his friend Staff that the best solution took some time to figure out and that most times, it was worth it.

Charlie arrived at the perfect spot, and his eyes were drawn to an object on the ground that stood out among the rocks and dried leaves. It was a slingshot made of a branch from a willow tree and a strip of leather. Charlie knew it well, because it was just like the ones he and his brothers used to make in Wyoming. They had never worked well, but Al had still carried his as some sort of talisman.

It was unlikely, but perhaps there had been a day years before when Al Berg had crossed this very spot.

Charlie smiled at the thought and pushed the object into Kip's saddlebag.

"Look at that, Augie. Your uncle Al may have been here, but I'm sure he's dead by now. I'd like to think he found a life for himself, but it's doubtful. Well, let's go get us some cattle, boy!"

Charlie crossed the river with Kip first to make sure Harold's herd could safely cross. He sure as heck hoped he wasn't crossing another man's land, but he doubted it; there wasn't a fence or any kind of marker. There could be Utes in the area, though, and if that were the case, he'd be in trouble.

As he crested the low hills, Charlie paused a moment, slightly stunned. There were cattle as far as the eye could see; the prairie was thick with em.

Charlie placed himself at the back of the herd and started running the cattle. He noticed running along with the herd were antelopes with big pronged horns. It was a beautiful thing to see—a thundering herd of strength and grace galloping across the landscape.

Moving the first batch of cattle went faster than Charlie figured it would, so he decided to take another run. He'd have to do it about four times, and expected it would get harder each time. The last runs would include the ornery animals that just didn't feel like crossing the river.

He took Kip and Augie to a nearby stream for a drink before moving on. Augie had taken a swim and was shaking off when Charlie felt the barrel of a rifle between his shoulder blades.

“Um, I’m not Max. We should get that out of the way,” Charlie said. Whoever Max was, he got some people mad.

"I don't care who the heck you are. You could be Jesus Christ, and it wouldn't matter—you're on my land." The man wore a hat pulled down low and a blue scarf around his neck, and looked like he meant business. "I'm Nick Turner, and I assume my no-good brother sent you this way.”

"I reckon you're speaking of Harold, and he doesn't know I came this way. I'm moving his cattle and thought this was the best place for them to cross the river. That bridge wasn't going to hold up," Charlie said.

"Where the heck did Harold find a cowboy like you?" Nick asked. He looked a bit like Harold, but his smile was less sinister than his brother's. "Most men would use the bridge cuz it's closer, and they'd probably kill a bunch of cattle. You’re smarter than most.”

"I appreciate the compliment, but it's just common sense to pick what works best—not what's easiest. I'm Charlie Berg."

Charlie amused Nick, and the feeling was mutual. It turned out the brothers didn't talk much because of a falling-out they'd had twenty years ago. Nick allowed Charlie to go about his business and even helped with some of the stragglers. He asked Charlie not to tell Harold they had met, because it was best that they completely ignored each other.

Nick left Charlie with a warning before he continued back to the stable. "Harold Turner is not to be trusted, Charlie. He's got a mean streak." His smiling face turned serious.

"I appreciate the advice, Nick, and all the help you provided. Burley is just a temporary stop on my way to Nebraska, and I hope to git before seeing Harold's bad side," Charlie said. He tipped his hat and took off. He hoped to get back to the stable before sunset.

Chapter Five

Charlie was hanging the last of the meat in the curing shack after soaking it in salt. It wasn't Charlie's favorite job, because he had bad memories of the chore. His brothers used to lock him in the shed back in Casper. It was cramped, stinky, and an overall unpleasant place to be.

Charlie was taking a canteen break on the stoop when Harold came by to pay him a compliment. "Charlie Berg, I was down at the barn and noticed a large number of cattle were close in. You got 'em across the river faster than any cowboy I've ever hired. Now I see you've put up all the meat. The day I nearly blew your head off when I mistook you for Max was my lucky day. Heck, you did the work of two men."

"Just doing the work you hired me to do, Harold," Charlie said humbly.

Harold handed Charlie payment for the day, plus a little extra. "Travelling alone, you must have developed some good tracking skills."

"Had to, Harold, if I wanted to keep food in my belly. What you are getting at?" Charlie asked.

"I'm still concerned about Max getting away with my money. I need someone to bring the scoundrel to me, or kill him, whichever is easiest. If I let him get away with it, then I'll have all sorts of no-good swindlers coming my way. They'll think I'm an easy target."

"Why don't you ask the sheriff to get involved? Not much else happening in Burley, so I'm sure he'd have the extra time," Charlie asked.

Harold shook his head. "It's quicker if you agree to get it done. Sheriff Sax is easily distracted, and although Burley is a mostly dead town, he has other things to do. There's the occasional theft, and brawls break out in the saloon almost every day. And, he drinks moonshine in between his official business. I know you want to get moving out of Burley, but I'll make it worth your while. If I don't hear from you, I'll assume you didn't have luck finding Max and moved on," Harold said with a smile and a tip of the hat.

Charlie was warned that Harold shouldn't be trusted, but he seemed like a fair man. Harold knew what he wanted and wasn't afraid to ask for it. So far, he hadn't done anything to make Charlie think he wasn't an honest man, although the moment with Katherine had seemed odd. He'd keep that in mind, but why not help the man as long as the pay was good and the work seemed right.

“I’ll see if I can find this Max you’re talking about. Does he have a last name? Can you describe him? Where’s he from?” Charlie asked.

“He looks a lot like you, but fatter with less hair. He's from north of here, and as far as I know, he don't got no last name. Heck, he probably made up Max." Harold chuckled. "You might have luck asking around town and see if he left any clues or if he made any friends in Burley."

“Did Max have a traveling companion?” Charlie asked.

Harold twisted his face and scowled. “I had a girl named Marylou who I suspected Max was sweet on. I caught ‘em whispering on a few occasions, and she disappeared at about the same time. I fear the worst happened to Marylou, because Max had a heck of a temper. An innocent man was killed on my ranch, and everyone pointed the finger at me, but I think it was Max. No one paid the price for the crime because there wasn’t evidence, and no one saw it happen.”

Charlie considered for a moment, then nodded. "If Max did something to an innocent woman, then he needs to be brought to justice. Augie, Kip, and I will head out tomorrow."

***

Charlie was fixing to leave the Turner ranch the next morning when a cheerful woman appeared with breakfast before he took off. Instead of a heap of leftovers, it was nicely arranged on a ceramic plate. Charlie had to think back to remember when he was served such a meal.

"Are ya sure this is meant for me, ma'am?" Charlie asked. Augie was looking at the plate and didn't seem to care who the meal was meant for—he wanted some.

"Mr. Turner wanted you to get a good start. Said you were doing something really important for him." She put down the plate and started to leave.

"Excuse me, but what happened to Katherine?" Charlie asked.

She stopped dead in her tracks. "She isn't to come down here anymore. She broke the rules by speaking too much to you. Telling you her name."

Charlie felt a slight chill at her words. Katherine had seemed frightened of Harold, it was true. "I'm the one who asked, and she was merely being polite. I'll feel terrible if I got her in trouble. Tell me that's not the case?"

The young woman laughed nervously. "Oh, no. She would never get in trouble for a little thing like that. Rules is rules, and all us girls know ‘em by now. Good day, Mr. Berg."

Charlie bid the woman goodbye, and then dug into his breakfast. When he was done, he pulled his scarf tight around his neck and donned a sheepskin coat. Drawing his hat down against the morning sun, he jumped on Kip and started out to find Max.

There wasn't a lot Charlie knew about the scoundrel, so he'd see what he could find out in downtown Burley.

Chapter Six

Charlie had just come upon a knoll when Augie suddenly began to growl. His hackles rose and he slanted his front legs like he was ready to pounce. Then, before Charlie could react, a huge skunk burst from behind the scraggly grass. Augie got a shot of the stink directly in the face, and the skunk scampered away with three small skunks chasing behind.

"You got a heck of a dose, Augie. It seems the animal was just protecting its young. I know you're embarrassed, boy." Charlie laughed as he spoke to his dog. He was glad it wasn't him, but it may well have been, because Augie went everywhere he did.

Instead of going straight into town, Charlie headed to the river where Augie could take a dip. Charlie knew it wouldn't do a whole lot of good, but it would lessen the stench. Sally Berg, Charlie's mother, used to make the boys sleep in the barn with the pigs until the smell wore off. The Berg boys would end up smelling like pigs after a few days, but it was better than smelling like skunk spray.

The blue sky was bright and clear, and Charlie watched a hawk circling high above. Like the hawk, Charlie's eyesight was unique, and came in handy when spotting danger in the distance. Charlie could see the bushes moving in the way that told there was a bear approaching. He could see a dustup from a mile off, warning a stampede was coming. Birds that would look like dots in the sky to most were clear and crisp to Charlie. He could almost count the red feathers on the tail of the hawk he was watching now.

He heard a slight splash, and turned to look at the river. Augie's head was the only thing showing as he sat in the murky river water.

"Too bad you didn't have a sense that a skunk was lurking nearby," Charlie laughed.

If a dog could turn red with embarrassment—Augie would have.

Augie still stank as he followed Kip and Charlie into Burley. Andy Mercer was sitting on the front porch of the mercantile. He gave Charlie a wave and a broad toothless grin as Charlie stopped to see if he had information about Max.

Andy took in Charlie's bulging saddlebags, packed with supplies for his quest for Max. "I see you're leaving like most who work at the ranch. I predicted such. Well, don't be looking for work here. Besides the Turner ranch, there ain't much work to be had in Burley," Andy said.

"I'm leaving, but I've got me a job, thanks. I'm looking for someone who used to work at the ranch. A man by the name of Max. Do you know him or where he might be?" Charlie asked.

"Are you here on Harold's behalf?" Andy asked.

Charlie nodded. "In a way, I guess I am. Max stole from Harold and may have committed murder out at the ranch. He also says a girl went missing when Max left. He sounds like a lawless scoundrel, and I'm getting him for Harold," Charlie answered honestly.

Andy crossed his arms. "Well, I'm not having any part of your business with Harold. I've heard too many stories, and I think Max was right to run out of here. Charlie, there isn't much left in Burley. Don't know how much longer I'll keep the mercantile open. All I know is I want to get out of here alive, and my chances are better if I don't talk about Harold, Max, or anyone who's set foot on that ranch. Harold has secrets, and maybe Max figured 'em out."

Charlie read the fear just under the man's forced sternness. "I'm not looking to bring harm to you, Andy. Good luck," Charlie said as he started to walk away.

He walked next door and got a similar treatment from Leo. Like Andy, he had an underlying fear of Harold Turner, so Charlie decided not to bother them further.

Charlie, Kip, and stinky Augie continued through Burley. Charlie tried to imagine the bustling mining town it once was, and it was sad what it had become. Towns like Burley were rumored to exist all throughout the West. They prospered then died, and Charlie wondered what happened to the old mines and the people.

His musings were interrupted when he reached the schoolhouse. There were no students at the moment, but he did see a figure inside. He tied Kip up to a hitch.

"Hello, my name is Charlie Berg. Mind if I come in?" Charlie asked as he gave a hand signal to Augie, telling his dog to remain outside.

The woman inside laughed. "I'm Clara Lanier. The smell doesn't offend me, Charlie. I've been teaching children my entire life, and I've smelled worse. Please come in. I usually have three students, but they didn't show up today. They are either ill, or their families have decided to move on."

Clara had a mound of white hair pinned into a swirl atop her head. Her eyes sparkled, and Charlie liked her immediately.

"What brings you to Burley, Colorado?" Mrs. Lanier asked.

Charlie told Mrs. Lanier his story about his sister and how he was eventually going to Nebraska. He mentioned Harold Turner, and noticed she winced slightly when she heard his name. Then, he told her he was searching for Max, and her face lit up.

Charlie was hopeful. Perhaps he had finally found someone who might have information about the mysterious stranger.

"So, Max has been here?" Charlie asked.

"Everyone who comes to Burley eventually makes their way to the schoolhouse. Out of curiosity, I guess, but they remain because I enjoy a good conversation." Augie curled up at Mrs. Lanier's feet, which she didn't seem to mind a bit.

"Do you know where Max went, and was he alone? I would appreciate anything you could tell me about him," Charlie urged.

"He had similar features as you, Charlie. A nice boy, I thought. Harold Turner had accused him of killing a stranger on his property and darn it, I believe Max didn't do it. I could tell from his eyes—he was no killer. There was a woman with him, but she clung to him as her life depended on it. She was not being forced like Harold Turner thinks."

"Did Harold come here looking for Max?" Charlie asked.

"Yes, and God forgive, me, I lied. I told him I didn't see him that day he disappeared. I didn't tell him about the woman. This town is scared of Harold Turner, and I'd sooner trust Max than Harold."

"I don't know what to believe, Mrs. Lanier. I am only going to find answers by finding the mysterious Max. Either he is bad, or Harold is up to something. Do you have an idea of where he went?" Charlie asked.

"Last I saw, he was traveling west." Mrs. Lanier poured Charlie a cup of tea while she spoke. A nice gesture to be found in dying town in the West. "I should note that the woman followed Max, and she wasn't dragged."

She smiled as she handed Charlie his tea, nicely sugared. "Now, about your dog."

"The smell is getting to ya, eh," Charlie said.

"Not in the least, but I have a trick that I've used in the past. I have an apple orchard on my homestead, and I do love apple vinegar. I also have more than I know what to do with. I'll throw a few ladles on Augie, and he'll be on his way to being stink-free."

Chapter Seven

Charlie pointed Kip west and started riding; he sure hoped he'd run into some clues before he got to the mountains. When he was on the edge of town, Charlie came across the Sheriff's Office, which wasn't much more than four walls and a roof. There wasn't even a door on the place. It had been torn off and tossed beside the shack.

Charlie jumped off Kip and walked up to the doorway, not expecting to see anyone inside. In the corner was a crude jail cell that held a dirty cot—the cage didn't look like it would hold a prisoner for long.

On the other side of the room were a desk and one chair. It looked like the other one had been broken into sticks and lay in a pile on the floor. There was no window, and it was dark, so Charlie's eyes took time to adjust.

Peering into the shadows, hey thought he saw a body beneath the desk. He looked closer, and sure enough, it was a body—a live body. Someone was sleeping under the desk.

The man suddenly woke, tried to spring up and hit his head. Augie growled and showed his teeth, and the whole thing startled Charlie, who fell against the wall.

"Get that gosh darn wolf out of my office! Who the heck are you, and why do you smell so bad?"

"I'm Charlie Berg, and this is my dog, Augie. He had a run-in with a skunk earlier, which was a whole lot worse before the vinegar bath. Who are you, and what are you doing hiding under the desk in the Sheriff's office?"

"I'm Sheriff Bob Sax, and I was taking a nap. I lost my rifle last night, or you'd be dead with your smelly wolf-dog," the Sheriff said.

"What kind of Sheriff loses his rifle?" Charlie asked. He called Augie to him, and Sheriff Sax sat in his one chair as he rubbed the bump on his head.

"I'd offer you a seat, Charlie, but I need this one. I threw the other one against the wall when a criminal escaped. I was napping, and woke up with the scoundrel walking right out of here," Sheriff Sax sighed and looked disappointed. "I threw the chair at him, but he still got away."

"I was hoping you knew of a man named Max and if you knew where he went when he left

Burley?" Charlie asked, not commenting on the Sheriff's choice of weapons. A man's got to make do when he's lost his rifle.

"Sure, I know, Max. He looks a bit like you, you know."

Charlie nodded. "I've heard it before. Harold Turner told me that he's a thief who kidnapped a woman and killed an innocent man."

Sheriff Sax shook his head firmly. "Not the Max I know. I'd challenge you to come across one person besides Harold Turner who thinks Max is one of them things. I drink too much, and I'm not the best sheriff, but good enough for Burley. Max helped me, though, told me to stay strong—no one never gave me a talking-to like Max. But far as I know, that rascal just wanted to make it out of Burley alive. He learned something. He was asking questions about the mine. Maybe thought there might be silver left in there that others had missed."

"Is the mine west of here?" Charlie asked.

"Sure is, and I'll tell you what I told Max. Don't go in there, because all the blasting caused the thing to collapse. Parts that isn't collapsed will be that way soon. Bad way to die from running out of air—I imagine, anyway, 'cuz it never happened to me. I'd be a ghost if it did." Sheriff Sax started laughing. "Who knows, maybe I am a ghost."

"I don't think ya are, but I do have a piece of advice. Find your rifle and don't lose it again. It seems like something a sheriff should have." Charlie smiled.

Sheriff Sax didn't offer a cup of tea as Mrs. Lanier did, but Charlie was glad he'd stopped by. Harold had convinced Charlie that Max was a no-good scoundrel, but no one agreed with him. The Sheriff's office was Charlie's last stop before heading out of Burley with Kip and Augie. He had to find Max and form his own opinion. If he was the good man the townsfolk said, then Charlie would continue on towards Nebraska.

Charlie felt well-rested as he started on the trail towards the old mine. He had gotten real sleep while at the ranch, which was a whole lot different from dozing with only one eye closed as he usually did while traveling. It was time to toughen up again, because he'd be back to spending the night under the stars—which he hoped to see for weeks to come. If a storm moved in and skies were cloudy, it would make his journey treacherous.

He looked at Augie, who was sticking near Kip and not straying far. In the meantime, it seemed Augie had lost his curiosity about what was underneath the brush. The skunk had taught him a lesson.

After people learned Augie wasn't a wolf, they often warmed to him. It wasn't unusual for him to be given a scratch behind the ears or thrown a bone. None of that was going to happen when he was stinky, and he knew it.

Charlie kept an eye open for scat, so he'd know if he was in a black bear's territory. He had gotten to know the bears in Wyoming, and where they kept their dens. He also knew which bison wallows they frequented and where they foraged. Avoiding those places was the obvious thing to do, but now he was in Colorado, which was foreign to Charlie.

As if his thoughts had conjured it, he had a snuffle just around the bend. Suddenly, a large brown bear stood before him, Kip and Augie.

"Well, I seem to have gotten myself in an ungodly situation," Charlie said out loud. The bear was on all fours and seemed as surprised to see Charlie as he was him. He remembered what Wenatchee had taught him: a ferocious bear only fears a more ferocious human. Often, shooting an approaching bear with a rifle won't work, and only makes them mad.

Charlie remained on Kip, so he looked larger than he was. He was higher up than the bear as long as the animal didn't stand up on his hind legs.

Charlie thought of how his own father acted when he was mad. Bill Berg seemed ferocious to him, so Charlie gave it a try. He yelled loudly at the bear, hoping to scare it from the trail.

But instead, the bear reared up, and Charlie knew he had to call its bluff.

Charlie kicked his heels into Kip's loins, and they charged the bear. It could have ended in the bear having a hearty snack before hibernation. Augie followed because that's the kind of dog he was—loyal to the core.

The bear took a sudden step back, then ran off into the trees. Kip jumped a log before stopping the chase, and Charlie lost his grip and fell onto a rock, hitting his arm in the process.

After making sure the bear was gone, Augie ran to Charlie and began licking his face, which also added an extra tang to his lingering skunk-smell.

Charlie smiled. His arm hurt but his plan had worked, and he'd survived along with the bear.

Charlie looked up from his spot on the ground and figured it was a good place to spend the night.

Chapter Eight

Charlie heard a crunch when he woke up at dawn the next morning. Sitting up to stretch and yawn, he saw his breath, and realized a hard overnight frost had fallen. It was time to bring Augie under the blanket with him, because they'd both benefit from the body heat.

He was moving northwest when he should have been heading southeast to avoid the cold. He had no choice, though, because he was chasing Max and not the warm climate.

The last clue he'd had was that Max had been interested in the old mine. So he'd headed that way. There wasn't a well-trampled trail anymore, so he'd know if a human had been by recently. A horse's hooves left a distinct path that was nothing like that of a wild animal. Someone else could have gotten lost in the unfamiliar area, but the mountains were his guide. He kept walking across the rough terrain.

As Charlie continued toward the mountain, he came across a different set of tracks. A human had been there. From the look of things, someone had been there in the last couple of days.

Charlie wrinkled his nose as a familiar scent reached him. They say dogs follow their noses, and that scent can carry them miles to find what they're looking for. Charlie figured he'd spent too much time with Augie, because he picked up a scent. He couldn't place where he'd smelled it before, though.

In the distance was a jagged rise, and Charlie guessed he was heading towards the mine opening. The trail picked up again, probably made by prospectors who'd flooded the area when silver was plentiful. Broken ax heads and other tools were abandoned on the ground, which were useless when the mine closed.

An area with no brush and no trees stood in front of the mine, which was no more than a cave opening. It didn't look ready to collapse, but it quickly became obvious that Kip would have to wait by the opening. The space was narrow, and Charlie would have to crouch down to go any farther. Charlie wasn't very tall, so he imagined some men would have to crawl inside. Kip was tied up to a tree in the shade, where he would keep guard.

Charlie and Augie had made several turns, and getting lost in the maze of tunnels was a real possibility. He wished he had a lantern, because the opening of the mine wasn't providing much light.

Suddenly, Augie's bark was echoing throughout the cavernous space. He ran ahead, yowling, and then stopped. There was an ominous silence, and it made Charlie remember the time Augie fell off the cliff in Casper and survived. Charlie wasn't so much worried, but he was baffled—what made his dog stop barking?

"Augie, come on, ya little rascal. Augie, A-ugie, come, boy!" Charlie called out.

He heard a sound like a falling rock and a yip, and his heart jumped. Maybe Augie was stuck. Charlie picked up his pace, but he kept stumbling over the rocks and uneven floor in the dark. "I'm coming, boy. Nothing is gonna hurt you."

Then he realized he wasn't alone.

"Take one more step," a voice said, "and I'll kill this dog and put a bullet in your heart. I knew that rat Turner would send someone for me. I ain't taking the fall for him. He shot that girl's daddy dead and was gonna blame me. I'd rather die than stand for what that scoundrel did."

The voice sounded familiar, but it was hard to place in the echoes of the mine. Charlie focused on the task at hand. "I just want my dog, Max. I'm willing to forget everything and go on my way to Nebraska. Let Augie go, and we'll walk out of this Godforsaken mine."

"Come ahead a few steps. I have a lantern, and I want to look in your eyes. I'll know if you're lying."

Charlie put his hands on either side of the tunnel and stumbled forward. All he saw was the blinding light from the lantern. Max raised it to Charlie's face.

"Either my eyes are playing tricks on me, or you're Charlie Berg. It's me, Al—your brother."

"Al? I thought you were dead. I knew I smelled something familiar, but I couldn't figure out what it was. It was you. But where's Max? Do you know a man by that name?"

Al grinned and pointed to himself. "I had some people after me when I was Al. Figured I'd give Max a try. It was working good for me until I came upon Harold Turner. I was set up by Harold, because he killed the man on his property. Marylou Sanders saw Harold kill the man, and I took her with me, hoping to tell Sheriff Sax what was happening. Sax was drunk, though, and not much use, as usual."

"So, you didn't kidnap Marylou?" Charlie asked.

"Heck no. She begged me to take her from the ranch and wanted to bring along her friends Dot and Katherine too. It was dangerous to travel with three others because Harold might catch me. I got Marylou home to her family in Denver and promised to free the others being kept at the ranch," Al said.

Augie was sitting by Al Berg's leg. He must have sensed Al wasn't dangerous and may have even known that he was kin.

"What do you mean about being kept? I saw Dot, as I think you are referring to, and she was smiling from ear to ear," Charlie asked.

"If the gals at the ranch don't do what Harold, says he locks 'em in a dark room with nothing but stale bread and water for a week. He also threatens their families. The gals are forced to write letters home saying they're happy. I don't know a lot about what happens back East, but I do know holding slaves ain't no longer legal," Al said.

Suddenly, a thunderous noise the likes Charlie had never heard echoed through the mine.

Augie disappeared down a corridor, and Charlie grabbed his brother like he used to do when he was a small child. Al had always been bigger than him, and he still was.

"Al, is that what I think it is?" Charlie asked.

"The mine is collapsing, and we're gonna die, brother," Al wailed. "No one could get us out, even if they knew we were here. This place is gonna run out of air. Augie was lucky! He probably died instantly by the falling rocks."

Al put the lantern down on a rock. "When the light here starts to flicker and goes dark, running out of air, so will we."

Charlie would not give in as easily as his brother. And, he refused to believe Augie had been killed by rocks. The wolf dog had run out just as the rocks began to fall, and Charlie would bet Augie had made it out. Heck, he might even be getting help.

In the meantime, they would stay calm. "We'll just have to dig out," Charlie said. "We were raised by Bill Berg, and we survived, so lifting a few rocks is nothing."

Al shook his head and removed his hat to rub his forehead. "A few rocks would be possible, but we've got an entire mountain in our way. We can pass the time before we take our last breaths by telling each other what we've been up to. You can tell me how ma and pa are doing. Do they miss me?" Al asked.

"Not so much anymore," Charlie said, deciding to humor his brother. He hadn't seen him in a while, and if they were gonna die, they may as well catch up.

Chapter Nine

"That's quite a tale, Charlie. Mom and Dad both dead and I didn't know a thing about it," Al said. He was less sad than surprised. Like BJ and to some extent Charlie, he wasn't too fond of their father, Bill Berg.

"Did mom suffer much? That poor woman spent years with a man she never loved," Al said.

"No, she got the fever and slept mostly until she died. Mom married dad, so she must have had some positive feelings for the man. She wasn't forced to join with him," Charlie said.

"She married dad because he offered her a way to get out of the West. He made promises and never kept 'em. Then he made sure she had babies to keep her put. If she were gonna stay in Wyoming all her life, she would have just married the man she loved—Stafford," Al said as he kept one eye on the flame.

Charlie was shocked. "Staff? That can't be, Al." Staff was one of the finest people he knew.

"Sure enough. Ever wonder why BJ didn't look much like Dad? I believe that that's why Dad was a miserable coot for most of his life. BJ didn't know, and I only learned it by accident. I never told, because mom wanted to take the secret to the grave. Since she's gone and we're about to join her, I thought what the heck."

Charlie kicked back and leaned against the rock wall. It was hard to believe, but Charlie was getting something he wanted and never had. He was spending time with his brother. It was nice, even if it took getting to life's end to find it.

"Did you and BJ hate me as much as I thought you did?" Charlie asked.

Al laughed. "Heck no. That's how big brothers act. I bet it served you well, and ya didn't even know it. We toughened you up, Charlie. The thing is, you were the strongest of the Berg boys because you stuck it out with dad. BJ and I ran away because we couldn't take it no longer, not because we were brave. Darn it, Charlie," Al said as he slapped his little brother on the back. "You managed to find me in a mine with only a few small clues."

Charlie felt like he had just found a pot of gold. Getting the approval of his long-lost brother meant something. "Thanks, Al. Do you ever see BJ?"

“No, I have not, but if I survived leaving Casper, I bet he did too. And what about Betsy? Ever hear from our sister after she married that man in Iowa?”

Charlie told Al all about Betsy and how he’d received a puzzling letter from her, how a man named Frank Taylor had married her, and he was a bad man. And how he believed that she had been taken to Nebraska and was being held against her will.

It was getting cold in the mine, so out of desperation, Charlie and Al held onto each other. Body heat worked as well as a blanket, and Charlie knew this for a fact, but Al doubted it. He gave it a try anyway. The men kept talking, because their time was running short. No use wasting time sleeping.

“Al, I know about Lisbeth Matters. I hear you were in love, but she died. Is that true?” Charlie asked.

Al tensed at the mention of Lisbeth. “Yea, it’s true. I take it you talked to her daddy.”

"I did," Charlie said. "Have you been in love a lot of times? I ask, cuz I'm gonna die without ever being sweet on a girl."

"Only the one time. It was the best feeling, but losing her was the worst. It hurt in a way I can't explain. Love changes a man, and I wouldn't be telling you this stuff if we wasn't dying. Men don't talk about love matters with other men."

"Don't worry, Al, I won't tell anyone," Charlie joked. "I don't think I was cut out to fall in love. I like being on horseback with my horse Kip beside Augie. Then I don't have to worry about anyone else."

"Nah, I don't believe that. You just never met the right gal. Doesn't matter anymore, though," Al said.

Charlie's eyelids grew heavy, and the next thing he knew, he jerked awake to find Al asleep and the lantern with no flame. He nudged his brother, who woke up and realized they were running short on time.

"This is it, Al. Will we just fall asleep and die, or will it be painful?" Charlie asked.

"Heck if I know, Charlie. I've never died before."

Sounds echoed down the mine walls, and Charlie cocked his head.

"I think the lack of air is making me go mad. I hear voices. Could be folks in heaven," Charlie said.

"I hear 'em too," Al said. "So, this is what it's like to die. I guess I'll see you in heaven, unless I don't make it there."

It was pitch dark, and the Berg brothers sat silent, listening. Then, Augie's barking cut through the darkness.

"Well, I guess old Augie didn't make it," Charlie said. "I'm glad to know he's in heaven with me."

They heard a familiar voice. It was Andy Mercer calling their names, followed by Leo and finally Sheriff Sax. Charlie thought everyone in the town of Burley must have died and gone to heaven. Nothing was making much sense.

"Al, do you hear what I hear?" Charlie asked as he gripped his brother's arm.

"I reckon our minds are playing tricks on us," Al replied.

A ray of light appeared on the western wall of the tunnel, and it slowly grew. A shadow appeared and lunged forward as Augie pounced through the opening and covered Charlie with slobber. Pastor Matthew peeked his head through the growing opening and praised the Lord. Mrs. Lanier could be heard telling Charlie and Max, as they called him, that she had hot soup and fresh bread waiting for them. Charlie and Al embraced.

What had started as the worst day of their lives had become one of the best.

Chapter Ten

Charlie pushed Al through the opening in the cave wall and followed close behind. The last thing he saw in the abandoned mine was a dead mouse. He and Al would have surely joined the dead rodent soon if they hadn't been rescued.

"Is someone gonna tell us how the heck you knew we was in the mine," Al said asked.

"It was the dog," Pastor Matthew said. "He came sniffing around, and I thought he was looking for Daisy. He started howling and running around in circles, and so I grabbed Sheriff Sax and followed the wolf."

Charlie rolled his eyes, "Dog, you mean."

Pastor Matthew continued. "We started following him, and word traveled. Leo had worked in the mine when the silver was falling from the tunnel walls. He knew the back opening was only recently closed from falling shale and limestone. We were able to get in from there."

Max grinned. "Well, I'm mighty obliged. And I'd like to let you all know, "I'm Charlie's big brother, if you can believe that. My family called me Al." The small gathering of the townsfolk nodded amongst themselves. The resemblance made sense, and lots of folks chose to use a different name every now and again.

"As Sheriff, Max—Al I mean, I need to know if you're a murderer and a kidnapper. That's the story Harold Turner tells. I haven't had a drink in nearly two days, and I'm prepared to throw some outlaws in jail," Sheriff Sax said.

"Sorry, Sheriff. You're gonna have to wait on that, 'cuz I ain't no criminal. I think you're gonna have to look over Harold Turner's fence to find the true villain. I got an earful from Ms. Marylou before I returned her to Colorado, and I aim to stop Harold's menacing. He thinks he's a king of this part of Colorado, and it's time we take him off his throne," Al said.

Charlie couldn't get enough of the fresh air, which was chilly as it came down from the mountains. Augie wouldn't leave Charlie's side, and Kip butted him with his muzzle. For a man like Charlie who hated to be confined, being trapped in the mine was something he wouldn't soon forget. Charlie vowed to take a moment each day to remember how lucky he was to live in the wide-open West.

Clara Lanier approached Charlie. "Since I don't have students at the moment, I wanted to offer the schoolhouse as a place for you and your brother to stay. You can figure out what the heck to do about Harold Turner. Burley isn't much, but we'd like to rid the town of scoundrels and outlaws."

"I appreciate that, Mrs. Lanier. I planned to head out of town, but I believe in leaving a place better than I found it. I'm willing to delay my plan until I can ensure the town of Burley is given a chance to thrive."

Charlie spoke with Al before leaving. His brother had agreed to help him free the girls from Harold's ranch and make sure he wasn't up to any other nefarious behavior. First, though, Charlie planned to visit someone he'd met that might help figure out what Harold was up to. He was going to ask questions of Nick Turner.

Charlie understood about brothers. Even after all this time, he knew things about Al just by looking at him, and like it or not, they'd always be connected. Charlie was lucky, because although his brother was a rascal, he was the good kind. He was like their father, Bill Berg, without all the bad parts. If Charlie guessed right, Nick had the good parts that his brother Harold lacked.

Charlie took the long way to find Nick Turner, so he wouldn't risk being found by Harold. He thought Charlie was hard at work finding Max, and it was best he keep thinking that.

Charlie pointed Kip towards a gully where he knew a water source could be found. Charlie needed a dunk in the water. He had begun to smell himself, and it was getting as bad as the slight skunk smell Augie still carried. He was sure Kip was thirsty, too.

Charlie arrived at the lip of the gully and gasped. To him, it looked like more of a steep chasm. Maybe it was being trapped in the mine, but it looked too treacherous to continue. Getting stuck again and having luck come his way again was unlikely.

Charlie looked down the ravine, and when he turned back towards the trail, he was stunned. He and Kip were shoulder-to-shoulder with an elk. It was a cow elk, but as big as most bull elks he had come across. Charlie scanned the clearing to his left, expecting to see a large herd since that was how they moved. Except during mating, elk cows moved together, only meeting up with bulls when necessary. The cow was alone, and while they wouldn't kill a human for no reason, it was darn intimidating.

The Shoshoni he knew thought highly of the elk, and looking in the animal's eyes, Charlie did too.

She grunted and kicked up dry dirt with her front hooves. The elk was upset, and that was clear. Charlie knew that even animals that ate only plants could charge and take out a man just because they were in the way.

“Hey girl, we aren't going to hurt you," Charlie said. He realized that Kip's size was intimidating, and he might be better off on foot. Charlie hopped off his horse and slapped his rump so he'd move out of the way. Before he trotted off, Charlie instinctively grabbed his rifle and a rope.

"Is that better? It's just you and me."

The elk's grunt turned to something close to a human sigh. Her head pointed towards the ravine. Charlie's gaze followed, and he saw an immature elk that he guessed was her child.

“That’s what you’re looking for. Well, little lady, you met up with the right cowboy.” Charlie turned and laid his rifle against a tree. "Won't be needing that."

Augie was sitting quietly the entire time. He seemed to be fine, leaving this one up to Charlie.

Charlie tied one end of the rope around a sturdy pine and the other around his waist. The young elk could get herself out with help, and Charlie could climb out after her. He rappelled down and tied the rope around the young elk's thick body.

"Okay, girl. I'm gonna climb back out of here, something I'm good at, then I'm going to pull you up. We're gonna work together and get you back to your mama.

Charlie made his way back up the slope. He wasn't sure where he got the energy to climb like he was a mountain goat, born to the jagged rocks and steep incline. He had just spent a day in a cave with hardly any air and barely enough room to stand. Maybe because it was an animal he was trying to save, and that made everything worth it. They were innocent creatures, not out to hurt humans, and Charlie felt he owed it to them to help.

Charlie reached the top of the ravine and steadied his footing. The mother elk stood back as if she understood what Charlie was doing. He pulled, and the small animal moved its legs—soon, mother and child were reunited. They paused and looked at Charlie with their brown eyes before running away together.

Chapter Eleven

Nick Turner's ranch was modest compared to his brother Harold's spread. It was hidden behind a hill, which gave way to pasture, and was beautiful in its own way. Charlie tied Kip up in front of the tidy, shingled house with a chimney that was blowing smoke. It seemed like there was someone home, so Charlie continued to the front door.

He pushed open the heavy door made of a thick slab of oak. "Hello, Mr. Turner… Nick, hello. It's Charlie Berg, we met the other afternoon by the river. Hello."

Charlie turned the corner and entered the main room with high ceilings and a roaring fire in the hearth. A kind-looking woman with black braids sat on a stuffed chair. She had a rifle in her grasp, but she didn't have a menacing look on her face.

"Charlie Berg," she said as she laid down her shotgun. "I've been hoping to meet you. My Nick mentioned he ran into a man that was working for Harold. He said you seemed nice, so I figured it would only be a matter of time until you figured Harold out to be the snake that he is. I'd stand and greet you, but I twisted my leg, and it still has a bit of healing to do. I'm Sara Turner." She offered her hand, which was a bold move for the lady of the house, especially since Charlie was a stranger.

"You guessed right, Sara. Harold sent me on a harebrained search for a criminal named Max. The criminal turned out to be my brother Al, whom I thought to be dead. He ain't no criminal, but he's pretty sure Harold is, which I have a feeling doesn't surprise you, Sara," Charlie said.

Augie brushed up against his leg, and Charlie realized he hadn't properly introduced his dog. "This is Augie, my dog, and he's not a wolf," Charlie smiled. He wasn't sure if the dog no longer smelled or if he had just grown used to it.

"I was going to say coyote, but it doesn't matter, because we're all God's children." Sara smiled, and Charlie liked her comment. It sounded like something his mama would say. With her black hair and olive skin, it looked as though she had some Indian in her, maybe Ute.

The door opened, and Nick came in from the prairie where he had been wrangling some stray sheep from his herd. He was happy to see Charlie, and greeted him warmly. They sat by the fire as Nick filled Charlie in on his brother, Harold.

"My brother Harold is a dangerous man. We both inherited the ranch from our father, but Harold proved too hard to work with. So I gave him over half the property, and we went our separate ways. But that wasn't enough. Harold wanted to control the town of Burley and everyone in it. He also wanted to begin mining again, because he was sure there was still silver in the mine. He started collecting unsuspecting girls from wealthy families to be his servants and to get money from their families. Mike Sturges at the saloon had girls, but at least they had a comfortable place to stay and plenty to eat. They may have been prostitutes, but at least they were treated like humans. Harold's girls were treated like dogs—they were his slaves."

Nick leaned back and shook his head grimly.

"He had the perfect scheme until your brother came along. He was on to my brother's misdeeds, and you know most of the rest," Nick said as he gently inspected his wife's leg.

"How do you know all this?" Charlie asked.

"I've sent a few men to work for Harold and come back to me with information. That man killed on Harold's property was kin to Katherine, who's being kept there. They were coming to rescue her, and Harold wasn't having that. He shot him cold and went on to blame Max for the deed," Nick said sadly.

Charlie scowled. "What you're telling me makes my blood boil. The thing about it is, I don't want to storm the Turner ranch with guns blazing and have bloodshed. We'd be better off taking what Harold has and seeing how he does without it. Then the ranch would belong to you again."

"I appreciate that, but I'm happy with the patch I have. Sara and I have a couple of boys, and it's a good size for what we need. The boys can handle the crops and the sheep. If they're happy, then we're happy. Sara is part Ute, and I'd like to give some of the lands by the river back to her people. We stole it from them, so it would just be returning what's theirs."

Charlie glanced over to see Augie curled up at Sara Turner's feet. "Looks like I made a new friend. I assume you'll be staying in Burley when all this is done, Charlie. Is that the case?" Sara asked.

"No, ma'am. After I leave Burley better than I found it, I'll be moving on. The purpose of my journey when I left Casper was to find my sister Betsy. That hasn't changed, and maybe my brother will join me in my efforts," Charlie responded. "For now, I'm gonna take this information and return to Burley. Things are going to change around here, and I hope I can count on your help."

Sara and Nick nodded in unison. "I speak for us both when I say there's nothing we won't do to restore peace to Burley," Nick said.

Augie barked in agreement.

Chapter Twelve

"Look at us, sharing four walls like we was kids. Never thought I'd see the day, Charlie," Al said. He and Charlies were resting the schoolhouse while Mrs. Lanier prepared dinner. She had insisted on feeding them, and said she enjoyed the chance to cook for company. Nick had come by as well, with a small bottle of something amber to share.

"Not what I expected either. Never figured I'd meet up with kin after I left Casper," Charlie said. "Thought every member of the Berg family was dead except me. And Betsy, I hope."

A mattress on the floor in the schoolhouse was mighty comfortable when compared to the cold November ground, and relief from the wind was something no man with a bit of sense would turn down. The wind at night felt like cuts from a blade.

"Mrs. Lanier's kindness is typical of Burley," Nick said. "I've made friends with most, from Andy Mercer to the Sheriff, even though we've had our scuffles. The mine closed and they lost almost everything, but not their spirit—they want nothing more than to have Burley survive."

Burley was turning out to be special. Al and Charlie owed them big for saving their lives and sticking with them to solve the Harold Turner problem. Clara Lanier made sure Al and Charlie had a place to sleep where they could gather. Together with Sheriff Sax and others, they planned to free the women at the ranch and loosen Harold's grip on the town of Burley. The Sheriff was joining Nick Turner and Leo Mackey to figure out a plan. Charlie had to find his way back onto the ranch without making Harold suspicious.

Mrs. Lanier called to the men from the potbellied stove in the corner of the schoolhouse. "Gather around the fire and have some stew I made special for you boys. Lord knows, I have no students to teach. I need something to busy my hands until some students head my way. I was put on this earth to teach, and I'm sad that I may have to leave Burley to follow my dreams. I'm no longer a young woman, so I'm counting on you boys."

"Yes, ma'am," they said in unison.

"Harold doesn't know I found Max," Charlie said. "I don't know why I can't just go back there and tell him that the man he was searching for died in the mine collapse. The only people who know about what happened are here in this room. I was a hard worker at the Turner ranch, and I'm sure I'd be welcomed back. That woman, Dot Fisher, might be an ally who I can convince to help me. I think Katherine is in trouble for chatting with me, so Harold will be keeping a close eye on her."

"I don't think that's safe, Charlie," Nick said. "My brother hates when someone figures him out, and revenge is sure to come. I won't let my sweet wife Sara anywhere near the man. He'd like nothing better than to hurt me more than he already has. My wife is precious to me, and I hate to think of what he'd do to her if he got a mind to." Nick barked a harsh laugh. "I'd be so mad that I'd have to kill him, and then I'd end up in jail, which I wouldn't like much."

"Don't worry about me, Nick. I'm not aiming to kill anyone or throw someone innocent in jail. I just want what's fair." Charlie shook his head, and his shaggy hair followed. "Fair isn't too much to ask, is it?"

"It is not, Charlie. It's what I preach on most Sundays," Pastor Matthew chimed in as he stepped through the door and joined them.

"Pastor, where's Daisy? Augie would love to see your dog," Charlie said.

"She's been moving slow, and I fear she's fixing to pass. I've never seen her in the mood not to follow me. It'd be a shame if I lost Daisy. She's my best companion." Pastor Matthew hung his head, and Augie's ears perked when he heard Daisy mentioned.

Poor dog, Charlie thought, he's got a bad case of puppy love.

***

Riding Kip, with Augie close behind, Charlie headed to the Turner ranch. He had faced villains back in Casper, and recently an angry mama bear, so he wasn't nervous about Harold. Charlie had learned it was those with the loudest voice who were the weakest inside.

He thought of Linc, who he had met on the trail. He didn't appear like much, but if he got mad, he'd be a whole lot more dangerous than a man like Harold Turner. Linc had the smarts that Harold would never have.

Charlie rode up the path towards the ranch house, remembering the first time he had approached. Harold had put a shotgun to his head until he was sure he wasn't Max. Having seen his brother Al, who Harold believed was Max, Charlie understood the similarity. Up close, however, he didn't think the resemblance was too strong. Al was about thirty pounds heavier, and older to boot.

At the sound of Kip's hoofbeats, Harold came down from his porch with a rifle in hand. When he saw Charlie, though, he smiled and laid his shotgun down. Charlie breathed a sigh of relief.

"I don't see that scoundrel Max being dragged behind you, Charlie Berg. I'm hoping that means he's dead somewhere, and you didn't bother dragging back the extra weight," Harold said. He had grown a beard since Charlie last saw him, which made him look more intimidating.

"Max is for sure dead, and I nearly followed into death, but I was fast on my feet. The scoundrel died in a mine collapse that nearly crushed me too, but I survived," Charlie said.

"You sure did, and I owe you for ridding this world of a bad man. Something told me I could trust you. I hope you're back here to do some more work for me."

"If you'll have me?" Charlie asked, rubbing his shoulder. It had been Nick's idea to put Charlie's arm in a sling, because he thought it would help convince Harold he had taken risks in getting rid of Max. Charlie's arm did hurt some after his encounter with the bear, but not enough to use a sling.

"Looks like you're hurting, Charlie. I'll set you up with a bed in the servants' quarters while that heals. I don't usually give ranch hands special treatment, but you earned it."

Chapter Thirteen

Charlie was in the main house, where he hadn't spent much time before. He was in a tidy room that had space for a bed and a small table. A basin of clean, clear water sat on the table. Charlie wasn't sure if it was for washing or drinking, but Augie appeared parched, so Charlie placed it on the floor like a dog bowl.

The sheets were clean, and there was a window open to let the chilly mountain air circulate. The house was quiet—quieter than imagined. According to Al, eight to ten girls were kept somewhere in the house.

Charlie didn't know what to do with himself. The sun had yet to set, and he followed its schedule most of the time. He wasn't sure if Harold would come knocking with his next work assignment. In the meantime, Charlie looked at the snowcapped mountains and wondered what kind of fool would make that crossing. Charlie couldn't see doing it, even if heaven existed beyond them hills.

Charlie was knocked out of his daydream by a pound at the door. "Yeah, come on in. It's not my door to say otherwise."

Harold Turner pushed open the door. "See ya haven't bothered to clean up yet. I'll have Dot fetch clean clothes. We must have had a ranch hand die on the job who was your size." He snickered at his little joke.

Dot was a name Charlie was familiar with from his time in the stables. She wasn't skittish like Katherine and seemed happy to be where she was. Al said he had spent some time with her, but he didn't say much beyond that. It was hard to believe Dot was being kept at the stable against her will. But Charlie was acting like he was satisfied under Harold's roof, so maybe she was playing the same game.

"Wearing a dead man's clothes is something I've never done," Charlie chuckled. "I'll wait for Dot, and after that I'll head down to the river to get the stink off me."

Harold frowned. "Icy cold water this time of year. There's a barrel full of water that ain't froze in the stable you can use. But before ya get fresh, there's some stalls that need cleaning. My next job for you is easy, Charlie. I have an urgent message that needs delivering. It's a day away in Denver."

"I can do that, and Kip and Augie are happier on the open range. I guess I am too," Charlie paused. "Not saying I don't appreciate the soft bed you're providing for the night."

Harold smiled. "No, I get it. Some people aren't meant to be indoors—guess you're one of em. And you're sure that Max scoundrel is dead?" Harold asked. "Don't want you heading off and then have him be coming back around, looking for payback."

"He's dead, alright. Buried in a mountain of rock that no man could survive," Charlie said.

"Good. I hope he suffered." Harold looked down at Augie when he growled. The dog was always a good judge of character.

Charlie was fixing to head down to the stable when there was a soft knock at the door. It was far from the loud thumping caused by Harold's fist. Charlie pulled open the door to find Dot with an armload of clothes.

"Welcome, Dot. We met once before in the stables when you were kind enough to deliver food," Charlie said.

Dot had red hair pulled back tightly and wore the same blue dress she wore the day Charlie met her. She was smiling, but her eyes lacked a sparkle, which was a shame because they were a lovely moss green.

Charlie was reaching for the clothes she held when he saw a bruise circling her wrist. When Dot saw Charlie notice the imperfection, she pulled her cuff down and dropped the clothes. Quickly, Charlie bent down to retrieve them.

"Thank you," the young woman said. "Please forgive my clumsiness. I'm sorry, Mr. Berg." Tears flowed down Dot's cheek. She was embarrassed, but also scared.

Charlie took a chance that he could trust Dot. "You knew Lottie, didn't you?"

Dot nodded, glancing down the hall. "What became of Lottie? Did Max take her to freedom?" she asked.

"Come in and close the door behind you, Dot. You can trust me, and Augie here ain't a wolf, so you don't have to worry. Lottie is free, thanks to Max, whose real name is Al Berg. He's my brother." Charlie went on to explain the situation to Dot. "I'm here to make sure Harold no longer kidnaps girls like he did you. If I do my job right, your families will be safe, and they won't have to pay that villainous Harold Turner any longer. He thinks he can get rich and open the mine again. He's sure there's still silver inside. If there is, it belongs to the good folks of Burley who are loyal to this town."

"So, you aren't working for Harold?" Dot asked.

Charlie laughed. "No, ma'am. Far from it, I'm just doing the right thing. I've met good people in this town who deserve a chance. Harold's plans are evil, and I'm gonna stop him before moving on."

The next day, Charlie was given the letter to deliver to Denver. Charlie carefully opened it and was not surprised at the contents. It was going to Doctor Josiah Fisher, Dot's father. Harold was demanding Josiah pay his life savings for the return of his daughter. If he didn't comply, Harold threatened to kill Dot. Charlie gave Dot his word that none of that would happen.

But the letter made Charlie even more determined to think of a plan to beat Harold at his own game and rid Burley of him forever.

"I expect I'll see you in a week. You'll get a package from Doctor Fisher, which should be returned to me." Harold took on a serious tone and pointed his long finger at Charlie. "If you run off with my return package, I'll kill you, Charlie Berg. I'll hunt you down wherever you go."

"There won't be no need for that, Harold. You should trust me. After all, I killed that scoundrel Max and came back to tell about it."

Harold didn't respond. He walked back to the house while Dot dutifully waited for Harold on the porch. Quickly, Charlie packed up Kip and took off with Augie not far behind.

Chapter Fourteen

Charlie stopped to share what he'd found out from Dot Fisher with the rest of his team. Sheriff Sax was going to dry out and deputize Leo so they could apprehend Harold once they caught him in the act. Harold had killed an innocent man, and they had to hear him admit to the crime. While Charlie was away in Denver, Al would build a real jail cell that would keep criminals locked up. Mrs. Lanier planned to visit the homesteads surrounding Burley and see if each family was aware that the school was still open. And Andy Mercer was going to go over his books and see if he could even afford to keep the mercantile open. Sara Turner spoke with the Ute people who were happy to help if it meant peace would come back to the area.

Charlie could see that Burley was a town that had the will to survive. Knowing a plan was in place, he set off for Denver.

Charlie pointed Kip towards a rise, and then it was prairie for miles. The last of the owls were heading for their nests far up in the trees. They hunted at night, but there were always a few that hesitated to head home to the nest. He thought hunting must have been too fun to stop.

The same thing would happen to Charlie when he was young and wandering in the woods—it was just too fun to go home. He was often with his friend Wenatchee, and they got caught out in the dark more times than Charlie could recall. It was cold and scary the first few times it happened, but then they grew to relish it. Being awake while most other humans were wasting time with their eyes closed was exciting. Back then, Charlie and Wenatchee felt like they were rulers of the land, which only lasted until their parents scolded them for being out at night.

Charlie smiled as Kip tried and failed to keep up with a small herd of antelope. He kept pace for a half a mile until the swift animals hit their stride, and then white tails bobbing and weaving were the only things they saw as the antelope pranced off into the horizon.

It was cold, but the sky was clear like freshly distilled moonshine as the prairie land turned rocky. Before Charlie knew it, the sun was high in the sky, and he and Kip were climbing crags in the shadow of the larger mountains. The feeling of being alone washed over Charlie, and it felt good. There weren't responsibilities for anyone but himself—and his animals, of course.

That feeling didn't last long, however, when he realized in less than a day he'd be in Denver, and then he had work to do. He owed it to Dot and the entire town of Burley.

But for now, the midday sun felt good on his back. He would enjoy the peace a little while longer.

***

Denver was bigger than Casper by double and couldn't even be compared to a place like Burley. It was the first time Charlie had been in a city—a place where everyone didn't know each other. It was also a place where a man could get lost, but luckily he had instructions to find Doc Fisher.

There was a town square of sorts in the center of Denver lined with storefronts. That was where Charlie was told he'd find a shingle with the doctor's name.

"I'm looking for Doctor Josiah Fisher. I have a post for him, and I'm supposed to wait for a return," Charlie said to the woman at the counter. "I'd like to deliver the letter personally."

"It'll be a long wait. The doctor is with a very ill patient," she said dismissively.

"Can you tell the doctor I'm a friend of Dot's—Charlie Berg."

A look of urgency came over her face. "Please wait just a moment, Mr. Berg. Doctor Fisher will be right with you." She scurried away.

Charlie walked outside and sat on the porch steps so he could watch the people rush by. For the life of him, Charlie couldn't figure out where they were going in such a hurry. Augie was alert and amused by the activity, but Kip looked like he might be sleeping under the tree where he was tied.

A red-haired man wearing a black vest and spectacles put his hand on Charlie's shoulder. "You're Charlie? How's Dorothy?" He asked.

Charlie took his hat off. "Yes sir, I'm Charlie and I was sent by Harold Turner to deliver this letter. I'm afraid the contents are unpleasant, but I assure you, Dot is fine."

He tore open the letter. "I'm confused. Are you here on Harold's behalf or my daughter's?"

Charlie didn't know how to answer the question. It would be easier once Doctor Fisher read the demand for money.

Dear Doctor Fisher,

Unless I receive $10,000 in a package returned by my agent Charlie Berg, your sweet daughter will have a deadly accident. I am aware *of your wealth and standing in Denver and know this will not be impossibility.*

Thank you

Doctor Fisher read the missive, and then collapsed to his knees. He handed the letter to Charlie, who took it but did not read it. He knew what the words said already.

"Harold Turner thinks I'm here on his behalf, but I'm not. Your daughter deserves her freedom, along with the other women on the Turner ranch. I need your help in making this happen," Charlie said as he helped Doctor Fisher to his feet.

"Of course I'll help. Who the heck are you, Charlie Berg?" Dr. Fisher asked.

"I'm just a simple cowboy who saw a situation that needed fixing. Dot is playing along with Harold, so I have no doubt she'll be safe until we get to Burley. She is a capable woman, and you should be proud of her. I wouldn't be surprised if Harold forced her to write this letter for him. He doesn't seem like the reading and writing kind."

"Tell me what to do and I'll do it, Charlie. And if we're going to work together, you should call me Josiah."

Chapter Fifteen

Josiah wanted to take his carriage to Burley, but Charlie convinced him otherwise. The wheels would be destroyed if they followed the path taken by Charlie on the way to Denver. Josiah had been educated back East and didn't have much exposure to life in the Wild West. He was about to learn an awful lot about it—including how to ride a horse.

Josiah rode his horse, Magic, closely behind Kip and Charlie and did fine until they reached a steep hill. Charlie had hardly noticed when he'd traveled this way, but Josiah pulled Magic to a stop at the foot of the incline.

"I'm not a cowboy, Charlie," Josiah complained. "I'm so sore that I won't sit comfortably for a week, and the thought of going over the mountain ahead of me is frightening. You will have to go on without me and present the package on my behalf."

Charlie thought for a minute or two. He hesitated to make the good doctor feel bad, but he had no choice. He had to coax Josiah to continue riding, so he decided to make him feel guilty about abandoning his daughter.

"I can go alone, but if it were Dot, she'd make it up that hill. She survived being tied up by Harold and placed alone in a dark room. That's what he does when a girl doesn't comply. You should have seen the marks left on her wrists as a result."

"That beast dared to lay a hand on Dorothy?" Josiah asked with fire in his bespectacled eyes. "I thought you said she knew how to handle Harold! I'll make it over the gosh darn hill if it's the last thing I do. And if I survive it, then I'm going straight to the Turner Ranch. Harold will wish he was never born," Josiah said. And with a whoop, he passed Charlie and Kip up the hill.

Charlie calmed Josiah down as they made it across the prairie and on to Burley. He made Josiah promise he'd follow the plan they'd agreed on at the office. Josiah would present Harold with a bag that contained worthless paper, with just a top layer of real money. When Harold looked in the bag, he would think he had the money, giving Al and the others enough time to storm the ranch and free the girls. They would tell their stories of being kidnapped and held against their will.

Charlie would get Harold to confess to the murder of an innocent man, and Sheriff Sax and Deputy Leo would be there to throw Harold into the newly built jail.

It was a foolproof plan.

"Think it might be a good spot for a rest?" Josiah asked Charlie. He was relieved that there were no more hills until they arrived in Burley, but still not used to riding.

"Sure, Josiah. You likely need some relief. Be sure not to travel far, because wolves and mountain lions don't mind this cold too much. In fact, the wolves thrive in the cold, because a lot of other animals slow down," Charlie said. The look of fear on Josiah's face made Charlie laugh. He had to remember that the doctor wasn't used to the great outdoors.

"I'm just going to run behind that tree over yonder, and I'll be right back. If you don't see me return, come looking for me. I might need help," Josiah said as he shivered.

Charlie inhaled the cold air and spotted a flake of snow. It was the first of the season, he noticed, and from the look of the sky, there was more than a flurry on its way. After matters were settled in Burley, he'd take to the trail again, and it wouldn't be easy in the snow. One thing Charlie was sure of, Denver not being a place he could wait out the bad weather. The busy way folks moved made him itchy, and the noise was irritating. He just might forge ahead to Nebraska next.

Charlie sat on a rock, thinking they'd better gallop on to Burley before the drifting snow started piling up.

"Josiah! Daylight is running short and it's best we get moving. Doc, you alive our there?" Charlie had meant the question as a joke, but after a moment passed without a sound from Josiah, he thought it may not be so funny.

"Josiah. Call out if you need me," Charlie said in a raised voice.

"Out…" Josiah's voice trembled.

Charlie grabbed his rifle from Kip's saddle and raced across the slippery rocks, just covered in the lightest dusting of snow. He followed Josiah's tracks to the brush, and stopped when he heard the sound of low growls. Josiah was standing in the clearing of the brush, surrounded by six wolves. They were in a pack, and they were hungry.

"I'm here, Josiah, and we're going to get you out of this. I know a thing or two about how wolves act, so just do as I say. First, don't run. You're a tall man, and that helps. Don't let their growling get to you, because they're just using their voice to tease you. I had brothers, and they did the same thing to me, but I know it didn't mean much." Charlie spoke calmly as Augie sat silently next to him, alert. "You're lucky, because your back is to the bushes."

"Shoot them, Charlie. I see you're holding a rifle, and that's what it's for. If I get bit out here, I'll die from infection." Josiah tried to compose himself, but he wasn't real good at it.

"I'll use my rifle," Charlie said, "but I won't be shooting any wolves this day." Charlie looked down at Augie and gave a nod. Then he pointed his rifle in the air and shot into the sky.

"Charge!" Charlie ran towards the wolves as he continued to shoot upward. When he had the wolves on the run, Charlie picked up rocks and threw them after the retreating animals. He encouraged Josiah to do the same thing, which he did with some coaxing.

Charlie turned back to Josiah when the wolves were gone. "You alright, Doc?"

"Not really, but I will be. You just saved my life, Charlie Berg."

"Nah, I've just been up against wolves a few times. Folks keep insisting Augie's a wolf, you know. I don't agree, but he's got a few wolf-like ways about him. You have to take over the alpha role and fight back. Show the wolf who's in charge. Don't work with all animals, though, so best you stick by me until we get to Burley."

Josiah wiped the sweat from his brow and pushed up his spectacles. "I can't wait to tell Dot about her dad's brave adventures."

Charlie chuckled to himself. If Josiah wanted to believe he was a hero for facing down a pack of wolves, there was no harm in agreeing.

Chapter Sixteen

Charlie and Josiah burst through the door of the schoolhouse just after sundown. It had been their goal to reach Burley before nightfall, because Charlie didn't think Josiah could handle traveling at night. Owls diving in the hunt at night can be unsettling if one isn't used to it.

Josiah pounced across the room when he saw a familiar face, and Dot smiled when she saw her father. She was sitting on a bench close to Al.

"Father, look at you wearing a sheepskin coat and a hat pulled down. You look like a cowboy, not a doctor."

There was never a prouder cowboy as Josiah beamed and hugged his only child. Tears filled her eyes as they embraced, and everyone looked on.

"Not to break up this joyous moment, but what in the heck is Dot doing here?" Charlie asked.

Dot stepped forward. "I climbed out of my bedroom window. Harold doesn't know I'm gone, but I just had to see Max—I mean Al. I had to thank him for alerting you that we were being held against our will. I have to climb back in tonight, though. If Harold realizes I'm missing, he might harm the other girls."

Charlie did not think Dot's escape was smart at all. If Harold realized the townsfolk were gathering against him, he might take desperate measures. Above all else, Charlie didn't want to bring bloodshed to Burley. He planned to help sneak Dot back on the ranch, and told Mrs. Lanier she couldn't draw attention to the schoolhouse.

"There's horses tied up outside and the chimney constantly blowing smoke," he said, "things Harold Turner would notice."

Al pounded his foot on the wood-paneled floor. "Excuse me, Charlie. You think you can come in here and lay down the law. Don't forget, little brother. We've all been here longer than you."

Charlie did not agree. He may be younger than Al, at just nineteen, but Burley needed someone to take the lead. And he was it. "I won't be here for long, but I'm trying to give Burley a chance to survive. I've seen what Harold Turner will do, and you have too, Al. We need to do this right, so let's do this my way, this once. I've got you this far."

Nick Turner stood. "Sorry, Al, but your little brother is right. The people of Burley needed a kick in the rear, and we should listen to his ideas. Let's not allow a family feud to take over here. I think that maybe if I had stuck around Harold for a bit longer…" Nick's voice trailed off.

Charlie and Dot made their way back to the ranch together. Charlie's arrival on Harold's doorstep would be diversion enough to allow Dot to sneak into the house. Charlie didn't blame Al for his outburst, because he realized his brother was sick—he had been bitten by the love bug.

It was well below freezing and the snow fell dry, dusting up in Charlie's face as he rode. By the time he reached the ranch, the hairs inside his nose had frozen. It was going to be a hard winter if he remained in Colorado much longer. The mountains loomed large in Casper, but they seemed closer and higher in Colorado.

He dropped Dot off behind the house and proceeded to the front door.

Charlie pounded on the door, and it didn't take Harold long to answer. "Charlie," Harold said, looking him over sternly. "You're empty-handed. Did you receive the package from Doctor Fisher and keep it for yourself?"

"No, sir," Charlie responded. "I have brought Josiah with me. He said he didn't trust me, and insisted on making the delivery in person. But he wanted to stay at a hotel in town, first, and have dinner."

Harold nodded, satisfied. "Come on in, Charlie. You must need a place to stay for the night, and I'm not about to make you sleep in the stables. Don't know how the horses survive night after night in the frigid cold," Harold said.

"I'll stay for a night, thank you, and tomorrow after I bring Doctor Fisher to the ranch, I'm heading out," Charlie said as Harold led him into his parlor. Charlie thought it was fancy treatment for a simple ranch hand, but he followed.

"Have a seat, Charlie. I want to tell you about my plans for Burley, and I think you'll want to stay when you hear me out. I've had a lot of men work for me, but you're different. You're young and smart, a good combination," Harold said, and then he scowled. "Don't go telling everyone I gave you a compliment. It's not what I want to be known for."

Charlie nodded and sat back in his seat. "It's not my intention to stay in Colorado, but tell me your plan. A man can change his mind." He wanted to hear what Harold had planned, and maybe figure out how to best stop it.

Harold told Charlie that he'd hired some prospectors to enter the mine through the western entrance that not many folks knew about. Of course, Charlie knew, because that's how he and Al had escaped. Harold said he had discovered there was a lot of silver left, and he was getting the money to pay men to mine. They would only receive a small amount of profit, and Harold would keep most of it. He was going to get so rich that he'd own everything in Burley. He'd kick all the people out of their homes and fill the town with his mine employees.

Harold figured his plan was working, because he was getting the first payment from Doctor Fisher. By selling the girls back to their wealthy families, Harold was getting rich.

In the West, folks got away with that kind of stuff unless a cowboy like Charlie wandered by.

When Harold was finished telling Charlie about his sickening plan, Charlie wanted to dive into the river and clean off. He felt dirty being in the presence of a man with so few morals. Of course, Charlie wasn't about to do that, because parts the river was frozen and the other parts were ice-cold; it would kill him in an instant.

Chapter Seventeen

The next morning, Charlie went for a ride on Kip with Augie following behind. Later he would head to the schoolhouse to fetch Josiah and bring him to meet Harold. But for now, Charlie needed to be alone so he could go over his plan in his head.

Charlie traveled east, to a more barren stretch of Colorado. There weren't many homesteads, because there were no trees and no water source. It was true frontier land was not meant for the faint of heart. The bison wallows were frozen, and there wasn't much brush for hares or other small animals to seek shelter. Charlie imagined that it was busy with herds of antelope and bison moving toward the mountains when spring was beginning to burst.

Charlie hesitated to go far into the frontier, as much as he wanted to see more. He still had commitments in Burley. Harold had agreed to meet them at the same rickety bridge Charlie had thought unsafe for the cattle, and it was time to set things in motion.

"Come on, boy," Charlie said to Augie. "Won't be long before we're on our own again. Feels good to be out here alone again, don't it?"

Augie howled, his wolf voice sounding clearer than ever.

***

Later that day, Charlie was surrounded by Al, Doctor Josiah Fisher, Nick Turner, Andy Mercer, Sheriff Sax, Deputy Leo, Pastor Matthew, Mrs. Lanier, and a few others that had been recruited. He told them what Harold had planned for the town of Burley and encouraged them to fight back with all their might.

"I know we're supposed to be lawless and independent. It's what sets us apart in the West, but no man should be able to just throw us out of the town we call home. Burley ain't much, but it's all I know. Been here since my ma and pa laid claim to the land I live on," Andy said.

"Same with me," Leo said. "I learned to tan hide from my granddaddy here, and my pa taught me blacksmithing skills. I wanna have a nipper who I can teach trades, and I want it to be in Burley."

"I know my brother Harold is mean, but gosh darn it, he's the devil," Nick Turner chimed in. "I'm glad my sons are nothing like their uncle.

Sara pleaded with me to break with Harold when we had nippers. She said she knew Harold was a dangerous man."

"Now, Nick, don't go comparing Harold to the devil. I believe every man has some good in him," Pastor Matthew said. Everyone else looked down, because no one agreed that Harold Turner had good in him. Pastor Matthew knew better than to argue the point further.

Mrs. Lanier sensed that things were tense and that everyone was cold, so she ladled some corn chowder into tin cups. It was so cold inside the schoolhouse because the fire was kept low during the day. The men gathered inside had agreed that the smoking chimney would call attention.

The men enjoyed some chowder and coffee, and soon the tensions died down. There was no time for fussing with each other. It would take all of them working together to take over Harold Turner.

They ran through the plan once more. It was almost time for Josiah and Charlie to meet Harold and Dot on the bridge for the exchange. Charlie and Josiah would take the wagon and some of the strongest men to the house. They would take the back way and free the women when Harold was occupied. Charlie hoped that Harold would then go back home, where Sheriff Sax would show up and throw him in jail.

"If all goes perfect, Dot will be exchanged for the fake bag of money. After that, you and Dot can go back to Denver and never have to worry about Harold Turner again. You can go back to being a doctor, and Dot can go back to living the gentile life to which she's accustomed," Charlie said as they rode the well-trodden path to the bridge.

"What if things don't go perfect?" Josiah asked.

"Grab Dot, throw her in the wagon, and go south to Denver. Don't look back and remember everything I taught you. If a pack of wolves come, you'll surely know what to do. You did good so far, cowboy. I'm not going to worry about you." Charlie smiled and gave Josiah a wink.

"What about you, Charlie Berg?" Josiah asked. The closer they got to the bridge, the more color drained from the man's face.

"Josiah, I chose to be a loner out here, and I got no daughter to be concerned about. I'm young, and you'd be surprised at the situations I've gotten myself into and out of. I ain't scared of a scoundrel like Harold Turner. What makes him better than me? We breathe the same air," Charlie said.

He said he wasn't scared, but Charlie was a little, which always helped to keep the blood pumping. Charlie was on high alert when there was danger involved, and with Harold Turner, there was.

"Look confident when you hand over the bag," he instructed Josiah. "You don't want him digging in the contents and find it's filled with paper. If you survived a pack of ornery wolves, you can survive Harold Turner."

The wheels of the wagon crunched as they passed over the frozen brush and dead leaves. From a distance in the fading sun, Charlie made out two figures which he assumed to be Dot and Harold. He and Josiah were done talking. In a matter of minutes, the first part of the plan would be finished. Dot would be back with her father, and they would be heading home to Denver.

Charlie pulled up before moving onto the bridge. He'd make Harold and Dot walk halfway. The crows were making a racket, which was an ominous sign.

Harold sneered as he got closer. "Doctor Fisher, I assume. I see your daughter is indeed worth a great deal to you. A trip to Burley and a bag of cash is proof of that. Take off your coat and lift your shirt so I can see from here you not holding a gun."

Josiah did what he was asked and stepped onto the bridge. Harold told him to place the bag on the ground in the center of the bridge. Then, he said, he would release Dot.

Charlie looked around, and didn't see anyone else but Dot with Harold. He hoped that meant he was alone, and that everything was going according to plan.

Charlie Berg understood most animals, even the unpredictable ones. The problem was, Harold Turner was a villain, and his movements were impossible to predict.

Charlie turned at the sound of a slight splash, and faster than a hare, two men jumped from under the bridge out of the freezing water. Another was waiting in the wagon to whisk Dot and the money away. There were two quick gunshots, and before Charlie could react, Josiah's arm was grazed by a bullet.

It happened in a flash so fast that even Charlie's quick thinking wasn't enough.

Harold called out as he rode away. "Thanks for your help, Charlie!"

Charlie helped Josiah back onto the wagon. Harold would find his house being ransacked by the others and he would discover no money in the bag, except for a paltry few bills. Harold Turner would be mad, and he had Dot Fisher.

And Charlie knew he'd take his wrath out on the innocent lady.

Chapter Eighteen

Charlie met up with Al and Nick Turner, who were riding in the first wagon. Andy Mercer and Pastor Matthew were riding the second wagon, with six girls in back. Two girls had been left. The men couldn't find them, and figured they must have been kept in a separate part of the house. Sheriff Sax and Leo had both retreated when they saw Dot with Harold. They didn't want to risk violence with the girl so near.

"What the heck do we do now, Charlie? I have to rescue Dot, and I don't really care what happens to me. I was in love before and she died, darn it. I'm not going to let anything happen to Dot Fisher," Al declared.

"After I patch up my arm, I'm going with Al to save my daughter." Josiah grabbed his doctor's bag and pulled out a knife and some gauze. He threw the supplies at Charlie and told him to remove the bullet. Using moonshine from Nick's flask, he gave Josiah a drink and poured some on the wound. Carefully, Charlie fished out the bullet and wrapped the doctor's arm.

"If we go in there with guns, lives will be lost. We need to regroup and come up with a plan. I have an idea, and it just might work because Dot is smart. She only needs an opportunity, and she'll run free," Charlie said.

"I trust you, brother. So far you've been willing to sacrifice for others, and I know you can do it once more," Al said

They headed back towards town and gathered at Nick Turner's ranch. While they rested, Charlie proposed his plan to the others. He was going to walk directly up to Harold's house waving a white flag—literally. As far as Harold knew, Charlie didn't know there hadn't been money in the bag. He could act surprised and mad. Claiming he knew how to get the money from Josiah, Harold would come to trust him again. Charlie would propose they drink to their newly formed friendship. Doctor Josiah Fisher had a tincture made of herbs that would make Harold groggy, and Charlie would put some in his drink. Then, Charlie would coax Harold into admitting all of his wrongdoing, with the lawmen listening to every word. At that point, Sheriff Sax and Deputy Leo could come in arrest Harold.

"Sounds like it will work if everything goes according to plan. Remember, Harold has men with rifles and who knows how many," Nick Turner said as he sat in front of the fire.

Nick's wife, Sara, stepped into the room and served tea and cornbread to everyone. Sara was part Ute Indian, and still had close relations with members of the tribe her mother was born of. Her sons had wanted to get involved in the plan, but Nick and Sara had forbidden them from doing so. One of the reasons Nick and Sara cared so much about Burley was because they wanted a place for their sons. They wanted a place the boys could raise families and not have to worry about violence. The same way her tribe had made peace with the townspeople.

Sara spoke up, her clear voice filling the room. "The Ute would also like to see Harold gone. I will ask them to stay behind when you approach Harold and be ready if you need them. With their bows and arrows, they'll scare the wits out of Harold just by being there. It is to their advantage if Harold no longer menaces the people of Burley. For years he has been harassing my people, as well," Sara said.

Nick smiled at her with pride.

"I'm not one to turn down such a generous offer," Charlie said. "I go tomorrow at sunrise."

Charlie spent the night in Nick's barn, which was his choice. There were animals wintering inside that provided enough warmth. Mostly, Charlie liked it because he'd be alone, which was best for thinking.

Charlie, Augie and Kip walked into the barn. Half the structure was devoted to the pigpen. Charlie had no idea the Turners had so many of the darn animals. Near a clean pile of straw was a pen with a mama pig and her piglets. They wouldn't survive in the outdoors with their pink skin and so small, so they were spending the winter inside.

The animals weren't bothered by Charlie's presence, but he hoped the piglets would stick close to their mama. Augie might see them as a special dinner treat. "Oh, my," Charlie thought to himself.

Charlie made a bed of straw and got Augie settled. He took the lantern to the pen before joining his dog for a brief slumber. Charlie fell asleep in the pen surrounded by suckling pigs.

The next morning, Charlie brushed off and went into the house before leaving for Harold Turner's ranch.

"How was your night. Little brother?" Al asked.

Charlie shook his head and smiled, thinking of the night with the grunting little piglets.

"I suppose I've had worse roommates."

Chapter Nineteen

Charlie held the white flag made of a kitchen spoon and towel in one hand as he Kip galloped towards Howard's ranch house. He sure as heck hoped a rifle wasn't pointed at his head. The Utes were positioned behind trees just beyond Harold's property line for protection if Charlie needed it. If Harold or one of his men put a bullet through Charlie, the Utes could shoot their arrows, but Charlie would still be dead.

Surprisingly, Charlie made it to the front porch without being shot. The front door opened, and sure enough, Harold was holding a rifle. And it was pointed at Charlie's torso.

"I was made a fool of, and if you was the doctor, I'd already be digging your grave. Since you chanced to come here, I assume you didn't know about the carpetbag filled with paper," Harold said.

"I knew it was filled with paper. Isn't that what you asked for—cash money?" Charlie asked. He was playing dumb.

"It wasn't filled with paper money, but worthless scraps. I hate being made the fool, and now I have Dot, who I'll never let go of now unless that Josiah pays me double and stands before me while I count every bill."

Harold directed Charlie with the barrel of his rifle to come in. "It gets worse, Charlie. While I was wasting time down at the bridge, some scoundrel came along and kidnapped six of the girls I had staying here. I told you how much those girls are worth."

Charlie shook his head in fake sympathy. "Harold, I came across a bottle of quality whiskey in Denver. Let's have a drink and decide how we're going to get rid of Josiah and get you his money."

"Well now, I think that's a mighty fine idea," Harold said, taking a glass from Charlie. "I must say, I think it's also might brave of you to come walking up here after I've been robbed from like that."

Charlie laughed, then stood and went to look out the window. As he did, he poured the liquid the Doc had given him into Harold's drink.

"Harold," he said, turning back to face him, "I've heard you're crazy with that rifle. I wouldn't risk coming here for anything else but to help you along with your plan. I got other places to be, but I thought lining my pockets with cash would be a good idea. I know where Josiah keeps his money, and together we can get it all for ourselves, and keep Dot."

Charlie kept pouring whiskey for Harold to encourage him to speak. "Tell me again about how you're going to take the whole town. I might have some ideas."

As Harold and Charlie were drinking, Sheriff Sax and Deputy Leo made their way into the house. They remained unseen in the hallway, where they could hear Harold Turner detail his dastardly plan. But the tonic from the Doc was strong, and soon Harold was fast asleep. When he began to snore, Leo and Sheriff Sax carted him off to jail. The few men on Harold's team who tried to fight were handled by the Utes. It turns out, not many people liked Harold, and the ranch hands did not put up much resistance.

Charlie raced to the back room, where he found Dot and two other girls tied to chairs with rags stuffed in their mouths. Charlie pulled out the rags, and Dot started talking after she caught her breath.

"I thought my days of freedom were over. Is my father alright? What happened to Al? Oh,

Charlie, it's so good to see a friendly face. Harold will come to check on me soon—we have to get out of here."

Charlie answered her as he untied her hands. "The only place Harold Turner is going is jail. A cell, built by Al Berg, who is quite the craftsmen, and Deputy Leo, who knows a thing or two about metal, that will hold him for a long time. Your father is anxious to see you again. We both felt terrible when Harold fooled us."

"You're a hero, Charlie," one of the other women declared as she was unbound.

"I second that," Dot said.

Charlie was not comfortable with the accolades. He had simply come upon a situation that needed fixing and fixed it. He knew there were creatures in the barn that needed his help, too. Someone would have to take care of them now that Harold was being taken off to jail.

Dot suggested Charlie take one of the horses, but he already had Kip. A man was only able to ride one horse at a time, and Kip wasn't ready to be replaced yet.

Nick and Sara couldn't take any more cattle or horses either, but legally the animals were all theirs as the only living relatives. So, they agreed to donate them to the people of Burley. It would provide the boost needed to keep the town alive. It amazed Charlie how the removal of one bad man could breathe new life into a dying town.

Al was on the front porch of Harold's house with Josiah to welcome Dot to freedom. Dot embraced her father first, who had risked everything to save his only child. His wife had died in childbirth, and as a result, he and Dot had an unbreakable bond. Josiah assumed she would come back to Denver with him, but with Al, that wasn't looking like a sure thing.

"Father, I'm sorry I worried you and took you away from your medical office in Denver. Your glasses are gone, too. What happened?"

"I lost them on the bridge when I thought I'd lost you. I only need them for work, and I'd say when I get back to Denver, I'll get a new pair. The thing is, Dot, I can't stand losing you again, and I doubt you're going back to the city."

"Does that mean you are staying in Burley, Father?" Dot asked, with a hopeful smile. Al had his arm around her waist, and they looked very happy together.

"I was looking around Burley, and I noticed something missing," Josiah remarked.

"What was that, Josiah?" Al asked, nodding knowingly.

"A doctor's shingle," he smiled. "Where Dot goes, I go. It took this near-tragedy to make me realize what matters in life." Josiah scooped up his daughter and gave her a tight squeeze.

"You won't get rich in a town like Burley," Dot said.

"With you, sweetheart, and seeing a smile on your face, I'm plenty rich."

Chapter Twenty

Charlie spent the day moving many of the horses to Nick Turner's stable. The Turner boys, Nicky and Stew, helped. The younger one was about twelve and reminded Charlie of himself at that age. Charlie told Stew that he was fortunate to have a father like Nick, and it would serve him well to stick around Burley.

Two of the horses were stallions, and as an expression of gratitude, they gave them to the Ute people. The Utes prized their horses and were grateful, so they gave the boys beads and some silver good luck tokens to hang around their necks. Charlie knew from his time in Wyoming that a relationship with nearby Indians was very valuable.

Later that day, Charlie headed to the schoolhouse to bid farewell to the town of Burley. He hoped his brother would join him on the quest to find his sister, but he doubted Al would leave Dot.

Charlie tied Kip up to a hitch in front with Augie moping behind him. Pastor Matthew lived nearby with Daisy, and Augie must have sensed that his lady love was not well.

He walked into the warm room, a fire now blazing in the stove, and was met with cheers. The look on everyone's face was a far cry from the first time he'd met them. Andy was playing the fiddle, Nick and Sara were dancing, and everyone smiled broadly. The town had carried a sadness about it before, but now everyone was happy.

Sheriff Sax clapped his chubby hands and gathered everyone's attention. "I think that we all agree that Burley would be nothing more than a few vacant buildings if Charlie Berg hadn't come along. He found me under my desk in the office when we first met. I'm sure he found most of you in poor condition, as well. Andy had no customers, and neither did Leo. Pastor Matthew had no one to preach to, and Mrs. Lanier had no students. Now we have the opportunity to change things because we don't have Harold Turner watching over our shoulders. I think I speak for us all when I say to Charlie—stay in Burley, and we'll make you mayor," Sheriff Sax said enthusiastically.

The crowd responded with cheers, but Charlie graciously turned them down. Burley was merely a stop in the journey to find his sister Betsy. He had no doubt that Burley would thrive. They had water access for crops and miles of fertile land. Harold's cattle ranch would provide work, and with services available, folks would move to Burley. Andy Mercer would have customers again, and Mrs. Lanier would have children to teach.

Charlie saw himself as a simple cowboy, and he looked forward to passing through Burley again someday.

The town was disappointed, but no one was surprised that Charlie Berg was moving on. They had known that was his intention, and he was the type to follow through on his plans.

Mrs. Lanier and Andy Mercer packed up Kip's saddlebags with food for the journey, and Leo made sure all his tools were sharpened. After many hugs and good luck sentiments, it was time for Charlie to leave Burley. Al walked him outside.

"I never would have come back to Burley and reconnected with Dot the way I did if not for you. Thank you, brother." Al laughed a little. It sounded strange, calling someone brother again after so long. "You understand that I've found my home in Burley, and I won't be joining you on your journey."

"I understand, and I'll always think of the time we had as an unexpected gift. Growing up, I never knew you, and now I can say I do. I'm proud to have you as kin, even if we never cross paths again."

Al kicked up the drifting snow. "Life's funny, Charlie, and who knows, we might run into each other again someday. Our big brother BJ might be alive, and Betsy too. Never give up on the Bergs."

"Nah, not after finding you in an old mine. And by the way, nice jail cell you built in the Sheriff's office. I stopped in and saw Harold. He got what he had coming to him."

"Sure did." Al laughed.

Charlie hopped on Kip, and with Augie close behind, made tracks in the snow as he headed down the streets of Burley. He smiled as Augie looked up at him, his eared cocked in a question.

"I know, Augie. We can't leave town without saying farewell to Pastor Matthew and Daisy, if she's still around," Charlie said to his dog.

Augie's ears perked higher, and he began prancing.

A weather-worn cross signaled that Charlie had arrived at the church. The structure was simple, and a strong wind might blow the whole thing over. Pastor Matthew was coming out an open door when Charlie arrived with Augie, who slipped past him and ran inside. "Excuse Augie. He must smell Daisy. Is she still with us, Pastor?" Charlie asked.

"She sure enough is. Congratulations, Charlie, because I guess, in a way, you're a grandfather." Pastor Matthew smiled.

Charlie tilted his head, and Pastor Matthew led him to the back corner of the church.

"Daisy had a litter?" Charlie asked, and it only took him a second to realize Augie was the papa. So she hadn't been unwell after all.

He smiled. It was hard to imagine such a skinny dog holding eight puppies in her belly. Augie sat proudly by Daisy's head as the eight puppies sucked at their mama's nipples. "That's what they were up to in the bushes. I was just leaving town, and I stopped to say goodbye. Augie sure won't forget Daisy, and I'm glad he got to meet his kin."

The Pastor grinned and nodded at the puppies. "You're welcome to take a puppy with you. They've had some days with their mama, and I trust you to care for one out on the trail. The townsfolk will take on the others without a problem, and I'll keep a couple."

"What da ya say, Augie?" Charlie laughed.

***

Charlie paused at a fork in the trail about a day out of Burley. Carefully, he adjusted the puppy wrapped in a soft blanket and tucked in his fur-lined coat.

"I think I'll sleep on it. We'll spend the night here and decide which way to go in the morning," Charlie said to Augie.

After setting up camp and a tasty meal of dried rabbit, they fell asleep under the stars.

Sometime later, Charlie felt a tickle on his face. He thought it was Augie until he opened his eyes.

"Nice to see a familiar face," Linc said. It was the loner he met on the trail on the way to Burley.

"Linc," Charlie shot up, and the puppy fell out of his sleep roll. "I've been in Burley and thought of you often."

"I see you added to your family," Linc said, smiling at the puppy.

"Yes, Augie met a girl." Charlie paused, and it didn't take long for him to think of a way to help his friend. "I was thinking, Linc. You said you were lonely and that a soft blanket would be nice. Well..."

With a grin, Charlie handed him the blanket-wrapped puppy. The puppy licked his face, and if Charlie wasn't mistaken, a tear rolled down Linc's cheek.

Linc cleared his throat. “Little dog got a name?”

"Nope, it's up to you. It seems like the puppy has found his new papa," Charlie said.

Linc looked up at the night sky. "Her name is Star. Thank you, Charlie. I can’t remember the last time someone showed me kindness.”

The next morning, Charlie took the right fork and headed towards Nebraska. He knew he’d probably never see Linc again, but he was glad he had left him better than he found him.

Charlie didn’t know exactly where he’d end up next, but he was sure that one day, he’d end up knocking on his sister’s door.

**** *The End* ****

FREE GIFT

Just to say thanks for checking my works I like to gift you
100% FREE!

Please GO TO

http://coolromancepublishing.com/gift/

And get your FREE gift

Thanks for being such a wonderful client.

Thank You

Many thanks for taking the time to buy and read through this book.

It means lots to be supported by SPECIAL readers like YOU.

Hope you enjoyed the book; please support my writing by leaving an honest review to assist other readers.

With Regards,

Sam Settle

Printed in Great Britain
by Amazon